Voyager:
a novel

Michael David MacBride

Also by this author:

- *Bidding Wars: Trading Futures* (a novel)
- *Emergency Preparedness: and other stories* (short story collection)
- *The Thompson Twins and the Case of the Missing Beaver Teeth* (mid-grade series, book 1)

DEDICATION

To those brave enough to set aside their dreams, desires, and lives for the greater good.

Cast of Characters:

Earth-based characters:

- Grover and Louise Baines
- Troy and Rose Baines
- Harper Baines (Troy and Rose's daughter; Baby Grover's mother)
- Grover Taft Baines and Clifton
- Grover and Clifton's children: Lyle, Adrian, Natalie, Chester, Horace
- Lyvia and Stacy
- Yasmin Torres (reporter)

Voyager 3 (1977) crew:

- Hugh Sullivan (born on Earth)
- Arnold Paul (born on Earth)
- Amelia Gardner (born on Earth)
- Opal Watts (born on Earth)
- Kirk
- Rebecca
- Sidney
- Eva
- Edgar
- Amber
- Maggie
- Kelvin
- Kacey

Voyager 4 (2001) crew:

- Isiah Heller (born on Earth)
- Zack Sheridan (born on Earth)
- Zina Watson (born on Earth)
- Nelda Crist (born on Earth)
- Jolanda Short (born on Earth)
- Mabel
- Bonnie
- Salvador
- Joanna
- Omar

Voyager 5 (2077) crew:

- Eloise Fisher (born on Earth)
- Alicia Wade (born on Earth)
- Ji Hennessey (born on Earth)
- Sanford Bostic (born on Earth)
- Yong Lipscomb (born on Earth)
- Jose Mason (born on Earth)

1—EARTH, 1979

Troy's father worked for NASA, which meant, for much of his life, his father was seen as a hero. No, he wasn't an astronaut, but Grover Baines was one of the men who made space travel possible. All the children on the block waved when he drove by, and when Grover was able to visit his son's classes, he was an act that no other father wanted to follow. Thankfully, the teachers realized this and were careful in their scheduling of father visits. Despite the adoration, Grover Baines was a respectful, thoughtful, humble man. He was happy to share as much as he could about what NASA was doing or his knowledge of space, and he would answer every question put before him, even if it was about how astronauts go to the bathroom.

"No, no, this is a very important question," he said. "Everyone has to go the bathroom, even astronauts." Then he'd explain how the urine evacuation system worked, and what happened to the pee afterward. "Well, some people think this is a little gross, but we put the urine through a centrifuge and create good clean urine distillate. Which astronauts are able to drink again as water." The seventeen children in the class scrunched up their faces and made disgusted sounds, but they were fascinated as Grover continued. "Water is heavy, and it takes up a lot of space. The one thing astronauts don't have, is extra room on the spaceship. And pee is mostly water. We just reclaim the water after evacuation and can continue the cycle for as long as necessary."

The students and teachers had never met a man like Grover Baines before. They were used to the type of scientist that was depicted in comic strips and the like: People who wore white lab coats, used impossible to understand vocabulary, and were aloof to "normal" people. Grover Baines wasn't any of those things. While he was dishing secrets, he was also slipping lessons into his answers and giving his audience something to think about. The "astronauts drink their own urine" factoid always killed (what kid doesn't like to talk about bodily functions?), but it was also an important lesson about how nothing goes to waste on space flights, and, more generally, recycling and reusing resources.

The most popular question he received was one he was unable to answer: "When are we going back to the moon?" Only twelve people had ever stood on the moon, and the last manned flight to the moon was Apollo 17, back on December 11, 1972. When he went to classrooms in the late sixties and early seventies, every child either wanted to be president or an astronaut or be both. But by 1979, it seemed like the possibility of going to the moon was unlikely, and interest in becoming an astronaut waned. Grover Baines was always quick to point out that people were going on space missions and doing important work, but he had to admit he didn't know when, or if, anyone would return to the moon. And Mars? Well, it would be amazing to have someone step foot on Mars, but that would require a major breakthrough in technology, not to mention an incredible influx of funding that simply wasn't there.

For all the talking that Grover Baines did about space, he spoke very little about his actual job at the space program. Had someone asked him directly, he would have answered the question. But no one did. The children and teachers loved the idea of spacesuits, doing spacewalks, and stepping on foreign planets; they were not as interested in computing launch trajectories or formulating new fuel for increased thrust.

Even his son, Troy, wasn't particularly interested in what his father did. He knew his dad worked for NASA, and that was cool, but Troy had no interest in following in his father's footsteps. He did, however, thoroughly enjoy astronomy, and this love for the stars was something that he shared with his father. The two of them frequently spent hours in the backyard staring through telescopes; family vacations often included visits to observatories; and, since they lived in Florida, they attended every launch possible (when Grover Baines wasn't working). Troy's mother, Louise, didn't have the same level of excitement about space as the boys in her life did, but she was always willing to indulge them. Though she rarely spent much time at the telescope in the backyard, she couldn't help but adore how her husband patiently aligned the telescope, adjusted the focus, and turned it over to their son so he could gaze at the stars, or planets, or galaxies. Grover and Troy could spend hours out there, and when they finally came inside they'd bombard her with tales of their discoveries.

In September of 1970, Comet Abe passed through the night sky. The comet was visible to the naked eye, but Grover and Troy eagerly gazed through their RV-6 Dynascope for a better view. This was Grover's favorite memory of staring at the sky with his son. At 5 years old, Troy was mature enough to understand what was going on but still filled with the giddy, uncontrollable excitement of a child. Plus, since he weighed hardly thirty-two pounds, he was light enough that Grover could hold him on his hip and guide his eye to the scope. Louise also had fond memories of that comet; though she didn't participate in the actual comet-viewing, she delighted in watching her boys bond and enjoy the sky together.

Troy and Grover were in the backyard in April 1971 when Comet Toba passed by, and again in 1972 when Bradfield and Kohoutek passed. They were in the backyard every January to view the Quandrantids, in April for the Lyrids, May for the Eta Aquariids, July for the Delta Squariids and Alpha Capricornids, August for the Perseids, October for the Orionids and the

Taurids, in November for the Leonids, and in December to view the Gemnids and Ursids. Every conjunction, and certainly every super conjunction, summoned them to the backyard, and, of course, every opportunity to view transit or occultation. They were in the backyard when Skylab was visible. They even tried to view the void that was Cignus X-1 after its discovery in December 1972.

Of all these moments, Troy's favorite memory was of Comet West in 1976. By that time, he was eleven and could fully appreciate what was going on in the night sky. He had been gazing at the stars and celestial objects with his father for six years and had begun to do his own research. Soon the child felt on the same level as his father—even though he knew he had a long way to go before he understood as much about space as Grover.

It was as they watched West burn through the sky that Troy casually said, "We should start planning for 1986, when Halley's comes back around again."

Grover hadn't given Halley's much thought; they had ten years to go. The last time that comet passed through, Mark Twain was just shirking his mortal shell, and yet his son had thought enough of their backyard stargazing to begin planning for something that would continue their shared hobby into his adulthood. It touched Grover in a way that nothing else about fatherhood had. To this point, the father and son relationship had been mostly unidirectional with Grover doing all the heavy-lifting. This moment, his son thinking ahead to 1986 when he would be twenty-one and he himself would be forty-two, was the first hint of what their relationship might grow into. Maybe they would celebrate Halley's with his son's first drink?

Voyager 2 launched on August 20, 1977. Grover came home from work that night to find Troy in the backyard intently studying the night sky. Rather than startle the boy, Grover stood outside the screen door and simply watched his son. As a father, he had always hoped his son might enjoy astronomy as much as he did, but he never wanted to force it.

When Troy expressed any interest, Grover was beside himself with joy but was always careful not to overdo it. Now Troy was twelve, and to Grover's pleasure, he was as eager as ever to know as much as Grover was willing to teach him.

Grover slid the door carefully and said, "Hey son."

"Dad, was there another launch tonight?"

"No, just the one for Voyager 2," Grover said. "Why?"

"I swear I saw something else go up, about six hours after Voyager 2."

"Huh, that's weird. There was nothing scheduled to go up after I left work. I would have been on my way home then," Grover replied "I guess didn't notice anything, either " He thought about it for a while. Troy was good with the telescope now and knew what the different launches looked like. It was likely that Troy had seen *something* if he was mentioning it. "Maybe they were testing boosters? Or a new fuel?" Grover speculated out loud, but even as he said it, he knew it was unlikely NASA would have done any of that without his being there.

"I don't know; it looked like something pretty big," said Troy. "I'm trying to find it now but not having any luck."

"Can I give it a shot?" asked Grover.

"Sure," Troy said, stepping back from the telescope.

Grover didn't exactly know where to begin to find the object Troy had seen earlier that night. Finding objects in the night sky can be elusive, even for an experienced night observer. Randomly searching the night sky through a telescope is seldom productive. Still, because he was a patient and curious man, Grover Baines scanned the night sky with the telescope. He didn't find anything. He could have taken more time to work backwards and reconstruct the possibility of a launch, where it would have started and its likely trajectory, and thus approximate its current position. But, he didn't. It had been a long day, and he was hungry.

Later, he would kick himself for not trying harder to find the object Troy had identified. It would have saved him many hours of pondering, because after that night he had a hard time shaking the idea that there had been a launch, and he had missed that memo. Or, worse, there had been some kind of launch or thrust test, and he had been intentionally left in the dark. But for now, his grumbling stomach got the better of him. He turned the scope over to his son.

"I'm sorry. I don't see anything, but I'll ask about it on Monday." He patted Troy on the back. "I'm hungry; how about you?" And then the two of them went in to eat.

When he got to work the next morning, Grover Baines remembered to ask around. No one seemed to know anything. Most of the people he knew and worked with had left when he had, so they had no additional information. It was possible that there was a night shift that was doing experiments; NASA was big enough and fragmented enough that Grover didn't know everyone that worked there. Hell, he probably really only knew fifty people or so, and maybe could identify another twenty or thirty by name if prompted, from the memos he received. If someone was doing a launch, and that was what Troy had said he had seen, then a lot of people would have had to be involved.

Eventually, Troy seemed to forget about the incident, but Grover didn't. It was one of those things that stuck in his craw, and until the day he died he never let go. He continued to dig when he had time, and ask questions when the opportunity presented itself. He kept a folder of documents in the bottom drawer of his desk of leads he thought were promising and memos that might be relevant. It never went much further than that.

On the day he died, Grover Baines woke up earlier than usual. Without thinking much about what day it was, he fell into his usual morning routine – shower, breakfast, coffee, and off to work. He drove the usual route from Bithlo to the Cape, down 520 to 528, across the Indian River on the Hubert H. Humphrey Bridge, and onto A1A. The 520 had always been a major route through that part of Florida, though it had gone under different numbers; it was renumbered the 520 in 1945. The 528 was relatively new. Grover Baines could remember when it was built five years ago. He started at NASA when he was twenty-four, sometime in 1968, and before the 528 went in, it was a bit of a chore to get from Bithlo to Cape Canaveral. That was the same year the bridge over the generically named Indian River was renamed after Vice President Humphrey to honor him for convincing the Air Force and NASA to help fund the widening of the bridge. Today, the drive to work was easy.

Grover hadn't always lived in Bithlo. Originally, he was from Escanaba in the Upper Peninsula of Michigan and had only moved to Florida to attend Brevard Engineering College. In 1962, when he was applying to schools, he read an article in *The New York Times* that declared that Brevard Engineering College was the "only space engineering college in the country." If it was good enough for the *Times*, it was good enough for him. Off he went. He said goodbye to his family, pasties, and winter, and hello to alligators, hurricanes, and the ocean.

One year into his studies, he met Louise Warren, and the following year they were married and moving into their new home in Bithlo. In 1964, Bithlo wasn't much of a town, but that was what the couple sought. It was near enough to Orlando that they could enjoy the city if they wanted, and far enough away that they didn't have to. For Grover, the best feature of the little house they bought was its proximity to what would become the 9,000-plus acre Hal Scott Region Preserve and Park and the stunning night sky due to the lack of light pollution from other cities.

Living in Bithlo meant an hour-plus commute to Melbourne (where Brevard Engineering was), and later a forty-five-minute commute to work, but the stunning beauty of the night sky in the remote town more than made up for the drive. Bithlo was far enough removed from other cities that there was hardly any light pollution (as it would be called later). Their backyard provided all the darkness needed for the stargazing Grover (and later Troy) could desire. , and they were surrounded by nature. Yes, this meant dealing with an occasional water moccasin or alligator, but it also meant being able to watch as bobcats, river otters, gopher tortoises, and bald eagles came and went. And, due to the remote location of their home, their backyard provided for all the stargazing Grover (and later Troy) could desire.

Now years later as Grover entered his building for another typical work day, he thought about how Voyager 1 had just entered the Jovian system and how near it was getting to Jupiter. The predictions had it arriving in early March, and today was February 26, and Grover had a nagging feeling that the predictions were wrong. Something told him today was a big day, and he associated that feeling with Voyager 1's closest approach.

So, here he was. He calculated the trajectories and doublechecked the figures himself and came to the realization that the predictions were probably correct. In fact, they were correct; March 5 was when Voyager 1 would get close enough to examine Jupiter's moons Io and Europa. With that out of the way, Grover's mind suddenly cleared, and he remembered why today was special. He actually had the day off. He wasn't supposed be at work at all. In fact, today was the day of the total solar eclipse, and he and Troy had made a variety of pinhole viewers to safely view it. Grover briefly lamented that had he still been living in Michigan, he would have been able to view the total eclipse, but the partial eclipse in Florida would have to do.

Grover checked his watch. It was 7:35 a.m. The eclipse was supposed to start about 10:35, peak around 11:48, and wrap up just passed 1:00. This meant he had about three hours, plenty of time for the 45-minute drive home. At worse, Louise, would laugh and call him an absentminded professor and maybe chide him for wasting gas, but if he hurried, he would have time to stop for donuts and still get home in plenty of time to watch the eclipse with Troy.

The Bithlo Bakery always opened early for the factory workers, but when Grover arrived at 8:30 a.m., there were still plenty of donuts to choose from. He took his time choosing a half dozen and was approaching the cash register when he heard a man's voice say, "Turn over the drawer."

Grover looked up and saw two men holding pistols aimed at the cashier. One was holding a burlap sack, and both were wearing ski masks. In movies, Grover had seen criminals wear ski masks, but it had been a number of years since he had actually seen a ski mask in person. People in Michigan didn't break out the ski masks until it was below zero, and only then if they planned on being outside for extended periods of time. By comparison, it was a balmy 42 degrees in Bithlo. Where did these yahoos even get ski masks in Florida?

The thought of ski masks made Grover laugh, which didn't sit well with the two men. They shot him. Both pistols fired, and Grover Baines lurched forward and then back as he struggled to control his legs. The box of donuts fell from his hands and tumbled to the floor. Surprised, Grover gasped as he, too, tumbled to the floor beside the pile of pastries.

There hadn't been a gun-related crime like this in Bithlo in a long time, and unfortunately, that meant the people at Bithlo Bakery weren't prepared for how to react. The gunmen fled, and the rest of the people in the bakery panicked. They wrapped Grover's bleeding wounds as best they could. Eventually someone thought to call the police, but by the time an ambulance arrived, Grover was dead at the age of thirty-five.

At the memorial, Louise couldn't bring herself to speak, so thirteen-year-old Troy spoke for the family. He didn't quite fill out the suit he was wearing, but he spoke clearly and eloquently about his father.

"Anyone who knows my father knows how important space was to him," Troy said, and no one in attendance bothered to correct him that it should have been "knew" because his father was now in the past tense. "But, family always came first for him. I was born on July 14, 1965, and even though that was the day that Gemini 3 made its first Mars flyby, my father was there with my mother as I was being born."

Afterward everyone would say how calm and collected Troy seemed while speaking, but inwardly Troy was shaking.

"On the day he was killed, my dad took the day off work so he could be with us and view the eclipse together. Who knows how things would have gone differently if he hadn't stopped for donuts, but he knew how much my mother and I loved donuts. He thought of us first, before even himself."

Troy paused because he needed to collect himself, but to the people present it seemed as though he had paused for effect. They waited attentively.

"My father was born on the day the Allies dropped 2,300 pounds of bombs on Berlin—he told me that—and my mother was born on the same day as Eric Clapton. Mom always says their birthdays should have been reversed, because Dad looks like Clapton, and she has German roots. Dad used to play guitar in college. Not as well as Eric Clapton, but definitely better than just a passing hobby. He used to play 'For Your Love,' for Mom, and it was like Clapton was doing a private performance. For their tenth anniversary, Dad secretly practiced so he could serenade Mom with 'Layla.'"

Troy took another deep breath to collect himself. After a few beats of silence, he looked out at those gathered and continued.

"Of course, there's plenty that Dad did that we don't know about—it's top secret. Everything he could share with us, he did, because that's how he was. He loved to teach and share, but he didn't overdo it. He didn't push his hobbies on me, so I got to fall in love with the stars and the sky all on my own. Once I did, that was a love we shared together. In fact, we are supposed be standing together in 1986 when Halley's Comet comes back around again."

He licked his lips; they were beginning to dry out. His throat was dry, too. He paused longer this time. He stared out again at those in the seats listening to him. People nodded encouragingly, coaxing him to finish.

"I guess I'll be looking at Halley's from down here, and he'll be looking from above, and hopefully our gaze will meet somewhere in the middle. I love you, Dad." Troy's voice finally broke as he wrapped up his eulogy and sat down.

When Troy and his father had first begun planning for the 1986 return of Halley's, neither of them could have imagined that planetariums would be hosting comet shows and offering guided viewings at the observatories. Grover probably would have suggested the family participate in one of these events to increase their ability to see the comet. It wasn't much of a drive to the Eastern Florida State College Planetarium and Observatory, and if they really wanted to make the event special, they could have driven a little further and made a mini-vacation out of it. Troy, however, intended to honor the original plan of sitting in the backyard with their own telescope. The view might not be as impressive as a larger telescope in a well-funded observatory, but it offered Troy a sense of closure and an opportunity to share his father's love of space with his own growing family.

Troy handed his six-month-old daughter to Louise and smiled at his wife Rose as he turned his attention to the viewfinder. Once he located Halley's Comet, he lifted little Harper up so she could peer through the scope into the sky. It's hard to know if Harper was actually able to see anything through the telescope or not, but she instinctively knew to close her other eye. Rose, Louise, and Troy all took turns gazing at the comet and commenting on how much Grover would have enjoyed the little viewing party.

Louise took one last look through the telescope and turned to Troy. "Honey, I have something to show you."

Troy handed his daughter to his wife and followed his mother inside. There was a cardboard box on the dining room table that hadn't been there when he passed through the room earlier.

"What's this?" he asked.

"A box of your Dad's things from his NASA days," Louise said. "Luke was," she started, and then changed directions. "Did you ever meet Luke?"

Troy's fingers played with the box's lid, but he didn't open it yet. "No, I don't think I remember anyone named Luke."

"He was one of the men your dad used to work with. Shortly after your Dad died, Luke brought me this box of things from Dad's desk. There were also a few folders in his car that the police held onto for a while, but eventually everything got put in here." Louise paused. "I don't know if there's anything really interesting in there. I've gone through it. It looks like projects he had been working on, and things he had on his desk. A couple old photos of us that are kind of fun. A drawing or two that you did. Anyhow, I thought you might want it."

"Thanks," said Troy. "I didn't know you had this."

Louise smiled at her son, gave him a quick hug, and then headed outside to be with her granddaughter and daughter-in-law.

Troy took the box into his old room and then methodically began to remove each item from the box, placing similar items in piles as if he were cataloging the contents. All child art was placed in one pile; there were four pieces, two in crayon, one in watercolor, and one a pencil drawing. Each drawing featured a father and a son looking through a telescope and some celestial object, or objects, dominating the sky. The photographs were placed in another pile; there were only two, one of Louise and Grover getting into a car decorated with cans and flowers after their wedding, and one of the three of them, standing on the beach. Troy was six. Troy had set up the timer and the tripod to take the family photo, and he was particularly proud of how it turned out. Looking at it now, the composition could have been a little better, but for six, it was pretty solid. The nameplate, Grover F. Baines, sat alone on the floor, as did a few other objects from his father's desk. Troy divvied the remaining documents and papers between three piles.

The first pile consisted entirely of what Troy determined to be "employment-related." Mostly it was boring HR forms, but Troy flipped through and read each of them anyway. The application was a neat little time capsule of who his father had been prior to NASA. Troy knew the high school, college, and graduate school graduation dates, but he hadn't known his father had such a high GPA. As a kid, he just assumed his father was of average intelligence. In part, this was because Grover Baines was a humble man who rarely tried to impress anyone and certainly never wanted to demean anyone.

Troy's perception of his father also had to do with proximity. Since Grover was Troy's primary exposure to what fathers were like, he assumed all fathers knew the things his dad did. Gradually, this illusion faded when other fathers proved themselves to simply not know many of the things Troy's father casually referenced. This was a fact Troy appreciated more and more as he grew up and became a father himself. Now, seeing that his father was literally the top of his class in high school, college, and graduate school, Troy was once again awed by the man who patiently changed his diapers, dealt with his childhood tantrums, and gave to his son as much as Troy was ready to receive.

Amid the other HR paperwork, one piece of paper stood out as odd. It wouldn't have been out of the ordinary for NASA to require a physical of an astronaut, but it was strange that they had required one of Grover—a man who would never step foot on a spaceship, let alone into space. In addition to the results of the physical, the form indicated a blood draw, and something that would be strange even for space-bound NASA employees, a "reproductive specimen collection." There wasn't much verbiage to explain the collection, just a box that his father had checked and a place for a signature, which his father had signed.

The second pile of papers consisted of memos, formulas, and notes reminding their author of things that meant nothing to the author's son. Troy read through each piece of paper and then turned to the third and final pile of papers.

These papers were easily separated from the others in the box because they had already been filed into a folder labeled "1977-08-20." The date immediately registered to Troy as the launch date of Voyager 2. Since its launch, space technology had improved exponentially, but still Voyager 2 chugged on. Troy briefly wondered how far it would make it with its comparably rudimentary technology. As the opened the folder, he half hoped to find some kind of secret about that mission. The voyager missions had always been Troy's favorites, and the fact that Grover Baines had worked on the Voyager missions definitely lent some nostalgic, emotional attachment to them that the later missions didn't have for Troy.

Inside the folder, Troy didn't find anything about Voyager 1 or 2. Instead he found sketchy notes from his father. He was sure they had meant something to his father but removed from 1977 by almost a decade and without the benefit of his father to decipher them, Troy was at a loss to follow the story the notes told. There was also an employee directory with thirty or so names highlighted in yellow marker. Four of the names had "astronaut?" written next to them. Other names, at least one hundred, maybe two, were highlighted in green marker; the name Grover Baines was one of them.

Of all the things Troy found in the folder, the most surprising was a copy of the form he had just seen in his father's HR paperwork; it was the "reproductive specimen collection" form, only this one was filled out with the name Tabitha Elliott. She had checked the box and signed the form as well. Troy checked the employee directory and found her name also highlighted in green. He stared at the form for a while, and then flipped it over. "Voyager 3?" was written in his father's handwriting.

Troy left the room and joined his family in the backyard, but his mind was spinning over the papers and the possibilities they presented. As his family chattered excitedly over the Comet viewing, he merely nodded at the right times and provided appropriate "uh-huhs" or "nahs." He was functionally there, but he was mentally still trying to decipher the papers.

Eventually Louise asked, "Find anything good?"

Troy shrugged noncommittally but quickly followed with his most complete response of the evening. "It was interesting to look through that; kind of like a time capsule. Mind if I keep the box?"

Louise was delighted to have the box out of her house.

In the morning as Troy and Rose were getting dressed, Rose asked, "Who's Tabitha Elliott?"

"Who?" He remembered the name but was pretty sure he hadn't mentioned it to his wife.

"Tabitha Elliott. Around two, I heard Harper fussing and went to check on her. When I came back, you were saying the name Tabitha Elliott and something else I couldn't understand." Rose paused and then added, "Something about a directory?"

"Oh," Troy said. "Must have been a weird dream."

He wasn't sure why he was withholding the information from his wife, and he immediately tried to correct himself.

"That was one of the names Dad highlighted on this old NASA employee directory."

Troy didn't want to go into the whole thing right now, and in fact knew they didn't have time to get into it fully before Harper woke up and their day got away from them.

"I'm going to try to call her and see if she remembers anything about Dad."

"Oh, a mystery!" Rose laughed good-naturedly as she walked into the bathroom and turned on the shower.

Finding Tabitha Elliott turned out to be relatively easy because her phone number hadn't changed. The only hard part was figuring out her area code, which wasn't included in the directory but had likely changed anyway since the directory was printed in 1968. Troy had worked as a telemarketer while he was going to school for Civil Engineering, so once he pieced the entire phone number together, he picked up the phone and dialed Tabitha's number without hesitation.

"Hello?" a woman's voice answered.

"Tabitha?" Troy asked. "Tabitha Elliott?"

"This is," she said.

"Hi. This is kind of weird, but I'm the son of Grover

Baines. You both worked at NASA together. Do you remember him?"

"Oh, I do. He was such a sweet man. You must be Troy. He always had your art work hanging on the wall." Troy could hear her wetting her lips. "I'm so sorry about what happened to him."

"Thank you. It's been a number of years now, but it still means a lot."

"What can I do for you?"

"I was going through a box of my Dad's stuff, and I found a couple things. I was hoping maybe you could help explain. He was clearly working on some kind of project, but I can't connect the dots."

"Oh! We were working on all kinds of things back then."

"Do you still work with NASA?" Troy asked.

"No, my job was cut during the transition to STS. I walked out with my things five years ago, in 1981."

"I'm sorry."

"I'm not," Tabitha said. "I mean, I enjoyed it, but I was ready to be done. Anyway, the question?"

"Right. Dad had an employee directory with some names highlighted on it. One was your name."

"Oh? We always did get along."

"But he also had a copy of a reproductive specimen collection form, with your name on it. What was that? It seems like a weird request from an employer."

Tabitha breathed quietly into the phone, and Troy waited patiently.

"It was. Very strange," she finally said, "and uncomfortable. But, if we ever try to leave the planet, they promised my descendants would be on board."

"I don't think I follow."

"They harvested some of my eggs and said they'd be frozen and put on a future flight into space. At the time, it seemed like a neat idea. I hadn't heard of anyone doing that, and honestly, it wasn't until the early 80s that I heard about egg harvesting again. They offered me a lot of money, well, at least at the time, and knocked me out. Did whatever they had to do, and gave me two weeks of paid leave to recover."

"Wow."

"Of course, then we didn't go anywhere, or do anything really with the space program, and it just kind of petered out. Who knows if they're still frozen where ever."

Troy and Tabitha chatted a bit longer, but then he was ready to wrap up the conversation. He liked the idea that his father's DNA was, quite possibly, in the stars always looking over him. Still, Tabitha's confirmation that NASA had collected "reproductive specimens" from some employees didn't necessarily mean that his father's sperm was on a spaceship somewhere.

Troy dug back into the paperwork when suddenly he was struck by his own memory of seeing something after Voyager 2 went up.

Voyager 2 was launched in the morning, and Troy distinctly remembered asking his father if there had been another launch later in the day. It wouldn't have been Voyager 1, because that didn't go up until September 5. Troy was certain he'd seen a second launch, and his father had spent a few minutes trying to find an object in the sky to confirm Troy's story. Troy even remembered some of their neighbors asking Grover about it. It was easy to see a launch with the naked eye in almost any part of the Florida but especially easy to see a launch when you're less than an hour from Cape Canaveral.

Initially, Troy remembered, Grover had suggested NASA might be testing a new booster, or that it was simply a test fire for the future launch, but neither of those possibilities seemed very likely because his father was on the Voyager team, and they would have wanted him to be there for something like that. Eventually, the memory of seeing a second launch blurred into the first for those who saw both. The idea that there might have been two launches was forgotten, but disputes over "the launch" persisted. It often played out with when one native-Floridian accusing another of early-onset dementia.

"Voyager 2 went up in the morning, you silly goose!" one

demanded.

"No. I saw it clear as day in the late afternoon, almost evening!" the other would insist just as adamantly.

"Are you sure you're not thinking of Voyager 1?"

"No, that was in the morning for sure. I remember that."

They'd argue on for a while before eventually agreeing that the time of the flight didn't really matter. Each had witnessed it, and it was amazing.

Troy couldn't know that Grover had spent much his final days trying to decipher what his son had seen, nor did Troy yet realize that now, years and years later, he was picking up the threads of his father's investigation.

Troy decided to try contacting a few more names on the list. There were only four names marked "astronaut," so he decided to start with those. He struck out with Hugh Sullivan, Amelia Gardner, and Opal Watts. Those numbers had all been disconnected. The last name he tried was Arnold Paul. He dialed and waited.

"Hello?" a woman's voice answered on the other end.

"Hello, my name is Troy Baines, and I'm trying to contact Arnold Paul. Is this still his phone number?"

"No."

"Do you know how I might contact him?"

The woman's voice was quiet, and Troy heard her sigh and open and close her mouth several times as if to speak and then pausing. Finally, she said, "I'm his mother, Grace Paul."

"Mrs. Paul," said Troy, trying to slow down his excited response. "Thank you." Troy wasn't sure what else to say, so he started rambling. "My father, Grover Baines, worked at NASA when your son was there. Dad was killed in 1979, and I'm just going through some of his things. I'm trying to find people that might have known him . . . to help me fill in some of the pieces of he was."

"I'm sorry. I really don't have any information for you, other than you can stop trying to find my boy."

"Oh?" Troy could sense from her voice that something bad had happened. Had Arnold died, been disowned his parents, or become a drug addict? He waited for Grace to speak.

"He died in 1977," Grace finally offered. "I don't know if he knew your father or not. But that agency killed him."

"I'm so sorry," Troy said. "I had no idea. If you don't mind my asking, what happened?"

It had been a long time since anyone had asked her about her son, and she was eager to remember him. She told Troy about how her son had joined NASA after getting his graduate degree in aerospace engineering. Arnold had loved the idea of space, of the space agency in general, and how excited he had been to get a job there. He hadn't cared about a salary, but the money was good. Arnold had lived at home right up until the end. He didn't have much of a social life; hell, his job was his life. All he wanted was to explore space.

Grace told Troy how over time, Arnold became reclusive and secretive, putting in more hours, defensively saying he couldn't talk about his work. Then one day he went to work and didn't come back. Grace called NASA and asked where he was. A secretary took a message, and then Arnold's boss called her back and asked if he could come see her in person. She knew the news wasn't good.

"Ma'am, I'm so sorry, but Arnold Paul was killed in a space launch on 20 August 1977. He was a brave man and loved space. I am so sorry for your loss," Arnold's boss had said.

"And that was it," said Grace. "He couldn't tell me much more. There wasn't much more to say. We had a memorial for Arnold, but it was small. Our family is small. Arnold didn't have any brothers or sisters. We didn't have anything to bury, but he has a spot in our family plot."

If his phone call with Tabitha had bolstered Troy's hopes that his father was onto something with an investigation into a secret third Voyager flight, his chat with Grace Paul all but confirmed it. When he hung up the phone with Grace, he returned all his father's items to the box and placed the box in the attic where it would be forgotten until Troy's daughter was old enough to stumble into it. By then the mission documents would be declassified and easily accessible through a freedom of information request, should anyone be so inclined to file one.

Harper would first have to grow up and give her parents time to fill the attic with her things from elementary, middle, and high school.

Rose dedicated one box entirely to Harper's much-loved toys and another to "memorable clothing," her first onesie, her school uniform from preschool, various shirts from various vacations and travels, her cap and gown from graduations, and so on. Another box contained Harper's school work from preschool to third grade; another from fourth to ninth; and a final box, which wasn't quite full, had her work from grades tenth and beyond—including her college acceptance letter, records of the first three semesters of the courses Harper signed up for, some college papers that found their way into Rose's hands, and each of the degrees Harper had earned.

"Mom," Harper had said at the time, "I'm not one of those people who needs to hang those on my wall to show off my accomplishments," and so Rose had simply tucked them away in a box and kept them. Here was a box of toys that Rose just couldn't let go of, and another box of toys just in case Harper ever had children of her own and they might be interested in them, and another box of toys that Rose simply wanted to keep at her house for when the grandchildren visited. If there were grandchildren.

Eventually, Harper would find her way back to the boxes in the attic.

"Jesus Christ, how much shit do you guys have in this house? Just when I think I find the end of it."

She approached the boxes with irritation at first and then tenderness, noting the care her mother, particularly her mother, but her father, too, took in preserving these memories. By now, Harper had a child of her own, and she saw these boxes of memories as reminders of the memories being made with her own child.

Sputtering through tears, Harper exclaimed, "Look at this

drawing I did when I was the same age as little Grover is now. .
. Look at this onesie I used to wear. Look at these toys!"

One day Harper would fondly remember the toys and
delight at seeing her toddler Grover putting them in his mouth.

"Oh boy, we really should have cleaned those first," Rose
had said, but Harper laughed and cried and said, "No, no, it's
fine. Just let him have fun."

And then, among those memories and boxes of toys,
Harper came across the box of things from her child's
namesake—the grandfather she never knew, except from
stories and photos. "What's this?"

Troy looked at that box and remember a time in 1986 when
he called Tabitha and Grace Paul, and how, even though it
seemed resolved, he still had a nagging feeling about the story
Grace was told about her son's death. He knew he hadn't seen
an explosion in the sky the day Arnold supposedly died in a
NASA accident. He recalled there was an explosion in January
of 1986. The Challenger. He'd also seen the 2003 explosion of
the Columbia. If, as NASA had told Grace, there had been an
explosion in 1977 that did kill Arnold, and it was anything like
the explosions of Challenger or Columbia, Troy would have
noticed. He had always felt certain of that.

And this how Troy, Rose, Harper, and Grover found
themselves sitting in a dusty attic late one afternoon picking up
the threads of a mystery that had already puzzled Grover, Sr.
and Troy so long ago.

As Troy began to tell the story of the two launches, the
mysterious contents of the box, and the supposed explosion at
NASA, Harper listened attentively, and so did baby Grover.
He chewed on a wooden Tinkertoy, and looked up at his
grandfather, taking it all in.

Finally, when Troy told them all he knew, Harper simply
replied, "We should do a FOIA request; what do we have to
lose?"

2—NASA'S VOYAGER PROGRAM, 1970'S

Making the case for space travel during an oil crisis was a difficult job; the easy way out was to not make the case at all. So that's what they did with Voyager 3 and its mission to the Alpha Centauri System. Internally, there were discussions. Plenty of them in fact, but with a very small team. Someone had to justify the expense, the secrecy, and the potential loss of life. Someone had to collect eggs and sperm and provide additional training, medical and fertilization-related, to the few adult astronauts who would be on board. Someone had to provide the educational material and the manuals to perpetuate the mission, and someone had to provide enough entertainment and leisure activities to provide for the ample downtime for those on board.

Publicly, nothing was said.

Part of why NASA's budget and staff were hacked and slashed every year was because the public had a hard time wrapping its mind around how to justify the expense of travel to the stars when there were hungry mouths on Earth. The collective public was excited to see a man on the moon, and they thought the images of planets and the like were beautiful and stunning, but ultimately the space program was expensive and, for the casual American, unnecessary. Moon rocks were neat, but how did that put food on the table, or find a job for someone, or improve the quality of life for the average American?

When the oil crisis began in 1973, and then peaked in 1981, the American public simply wouldn't tolerate the idea that NASA was wasting thousands, or millions, of gallons of gasoline to launch rockets into space. This was a matter that Grover Baines complained to his family about regularly.

He rarely brought his work home, but when he did, it often began with, "The public just doesn't understand" and then typically went down the road of explaining how rocket fuel is different from gasoline. NASA was using RP-1, which is essentially highly-refined kerosene, but it didn't matter to the public that NASA wasn't using gasoline. What mattered was a perceived waste by NASA when many Americans couldn't afford a tank of gas to get to work. Eventually, the angry calls and letters to politicians made an impact as representatives weighed in on the budget and voted to cut the space program funding. Consequently, there were only eight manned flights from 1971-1980. There were zero flights in 1974, one in 1975, and then none until 1981 when the Space Transportation System (STS) took its maiden flight on April 12, 1981.

The STS program began as a plan in 1969 to create a reusable space transportation system. Grover, new to NASA in 1968, applied to be part of the STS team as soon as he heard about it. Reusable craft was something he believed strongly in, but his superiors informed him he was vital where he was, and his application was denied.

As with most things involving any kind of bureaucracy, the start of the program was delayed for almost three years and kept from the public view for almost a decade. It wasn't until Columbia took its test flight years later that the world was reintroduced to what NASA had been working on for the last decade.

Unfortunately, that gap in the timeline was enough to cause a generation of children to grow up with no burning desire to become astronauts. Even Troy, who grew up with a NASA scientist as a father, who had plenty of exposure to the space program, and who loved the stars and the sky, never considered becoming an astronaut.

Without much public interest or the push of youngsters clamoring to replace its aging astronauts, NASA's funding and staff continued to shrink, never to return to the glory days of when it accounted for 4.41% of the national budget.

The Mariner Jupiter/Saturn program, later renamed the Voyager program, began on July 1, 1972. At that time, NASA had made a strong case to President Nixon for the value of the program. NASA had leaned heavily on the "once-in-every-176-years" alignment of the planets that would occur in 1977, which would allow the craft to use a gravity-assisted slingshot that would shave decades off the predicted length of flight to the gas giants.

Nixon wasn't convinced until a NASA official challenged him with the claim, "Kennedy would have done it."

It didn't take Nixon long to reply. "Well, let's do two of them then," and Voyager 1 and 2 were funded. The approved funding, however, didn't mean the project team was guaranteed any longevity of the program. Apollo 18, 19, and 20, all extended-lunar-stay missions had been cancelled just two years prior, and there was no promise to replace the cancelled Apollo program with another manned exploratory one.

Missions such as Voyager 3's had been under consideration since the heyday of the Space Race, but with each passing year of shrinking budgets and diminished staff, any manned mission to Mars and beyond was pushed off indefinitely. However, a small contingent of scientists, call them NASA rebels if you will, decided that before its budget and staff disappeared entirely, NASA would launch the one mission that really mattered: The Alpha Centauri System.

This small dedicated team was pretty certain there was no other life within their solar system, but they longed to know if there was life or life-sustaining resources in a nearby system. If the oil crisis was going to continue crippling life on Earth, everyone would benefit from alternative energy sources from "out there." These scientists were each aware of the fact that none of them would live to reap the benefits of this mission, but if even a small group of humans thrived from their efforts, it would be considered a success.

In 1974, NASA's budget dropped to less than half of what it had been in 1968. Budget cuts had become increasingly jarring, and each successive year was worse and worse, until it finally hit bottom in 1975. By then, the small Voyager 3 team was convinced there wouldn't be a space program much longer and believed it had no choice but to execute the plan as soon as possible if they were going to launch the mission.

The secret Voyager 3 team couldn't afford to dip into the official Voyager budget to create a third craft, so they took an old prototype and decided to retrofit it for the mission. To keep information leaks to a minimum, the team proceeded with a skeletal crew of four, which meant each of the humans on board had to be an expert in several fields. Each person had to be young, in good health with good genes, and well educated. Additionally, the team opted for people who were so dedicated to their education and space exploration that they were effectively loners, which would further isolate the mission from curious inquiries. They settled on two men, Hugh Sullivan and Arnold Paul, and two women, Amelia Gardner and Opal Watts.

Hugh Sullivan and Arnold Paul were stereotypical bachelors. Hugh lived alone in an apartment, and Arnold lived with his mother. When asked about girlfriends or wives, they would simply shrug and say, "Who has time for all that?" This was the answer their interviewers were looking for. Neither Hugh nor Arnold knew it when they first agreed to be part of Voyager 3, but their sexual preference might have been considered an asset for the mission. The team putting together the Voyager 3 mission saw procreative affairs as potentially dangerous to the mission.

Given the restrictive movement and close confines with no opportunity to separate from one another for the rest of their lives, any avoidable relational friction was to be eliminated at all costs. The craft was going to be loaded with reproductive specimens from a couple hundred NASA employees, and so Hugh and Arnold would not have been expected to help populate the craft or the new colony. It was concerning that the female astronauts might form maternal bonds with their artificially inseminated offspring, but there simply wasn't a way around that. In retrospect, Hugh and Arnold could have bested Sally Ride to the punch by six years by becoming the first LGBT astronauts, but the fear of homophobia was too great.

Voyager 2 launched at 14:29:00 UTC (9:29 a.m. EST) on August 20, 1977, and Voyager 3 went up nearly eight hours later. It would have been impossible to hide a second launch, so they didn't even try. They waited until there were fewer people around, and then pulled the trigger assuming that forgiveness would be easier to get than permission. They also knew that they had two things working in their favor. First, rocket, booster, and fuel tests were fairly common. Second, it was generally known that Voyager 1 was going to launch after Voyager 2, but it was not well-known as to how much later that would be. If anyone happened to notice the Voyager 3 launch, they might think, "Oh, there goes Voyager 1." If they knew when Voyager 1 was supposed to launch and happened to see Voyager 3 go up, then they might think, "Oh, they're doing a booster test for Voyager 1." It seemed easily enough to create the confusion that could cover the covert launch.

Once Voyager 3 was clear of the atmosphere, it quickly out-paced Voyager 2.

Voyager 1 launched September 5, 1977, and because it was on a quicker trajectory, it lapped Voyager 2. By that time, Voyager 3 was already well on its way and both of its smaller unmanned brothers were in its rearview (well, figuratively, because it didn't actually have one). Since no one was looking for a spacecraft deeper in space than Voyager 1, no one noticed Voyager 3. Why would they? Even if they had noticed it, they might not have come to the conclusion that NASA had launched a manned spaceship without notifying the public. Had someone seen the object, they might have attributed it to some other obsolete probe; they definitely wouldn't have known it contained four astronauts.

Yet, there they were.

Hugh Sullivan, the senior crew member, slid under NASA's age requirement by four years. He was a pilot in the Air Force and a geneticist by training. Hugh graduated from high school in 1958 and attended University of Wisconsin, at Madison, for both undergrad and graduate school. He studied under James F. Crow, whose cutting-edge work in genetics was hugely influential to Hugh's own projects. Hugh even had the honor of attending an externship held by Enos J. Perry while visiting at Rutgers.

Perry taught Hugh how to freeze and thaw bovine semen. It blew Hugh's mind to think that life on that level could be put into a state of frozen animation and then brought back at the whim of a scientist and still create viable life. Hugh visited the sperm banks that were created in the 1920s at the University of Iowa and spent hours upon hours in the lab working with fruit flies to track genetic mutation through the generations. It helped that fruit flies only lived, on the outside, fifty days, and that meant that in the course of a year, he could observe fifty generations of adaptation and mutation. Hugh packed as much into his education as he could, and as soon as he graduated, he applied for NASA.

The age gap between Hugh and Amelia Gardner was eleven years. Even though both spent time at the University of Iowa, their paths had never crossed before the mission. Amelia didn't come from a lifelong desire to be a pilot or an astronaut. She was an excellent student who loved to read, and it was her reading that actually determined her career path.

Amelia had been assigned an "informative essay" project in one of her classes. Most students typically picked a topic they were already familiar with and finished the paper in short order, but Amelia delayed choosing a topic until something really piqued her interest. It happened one day while she was reading about an unnamed woman in 1884 who conceived the first child from artificial insemination. Amelia had read reports about artificial insemination before, but she had no idea it dated back as far as before the turn of the century. Yet, here it was.

An unnamed woman had been given chloroform to render her unconscious before Dr. Pancoast inserted semen collected from one of his medical students (the most attractive one, in the doctor's opinion anyway) into the woman via a syringe, and then carefully packed her cervix with gauze. Later, Pancoast told the woman's husband about what had been done, but they never told the woman. The six medical students who observed the procedure were sworn to secrecy, and they remained mum until 1909 when one student broke his silence.

Amelia was equal parts shocked and amazed by the story; not only had she found her muse for her informative essay, but she also found her calling. She finished her program at the University of Iowa, and then pursued her graduate degree at Manchester where she worked under Robert Edwards and Patrick Steptoe at Oldham Hospital who were both attempting to perfect in vitro fertilization. They hoped to extend the possibility of giving birth for women who were otherwise infertile and would eventually prove success with the birth of Louise Joy Brown on July 25, 1978. By then, Amelia was already hurtling through space.

Amelia was the only astronaut on board Voyager 3 who was not a pilot. She had been selected on the strength of her IVF background and artificial insemination skills alone. Amelia was confident in the IVF procedure, but if for some reason her technique didn't work, there was always the backup plan of simply using the time-tested method of artificial insemination of the two female astronauts. Both female crew members, Amelia and Opal, had been tested for fertility prior to the mission. While the use of frozen eggs collected from NASA employees was preferred for diversity in the gene pool of the astronauts born on Voyager 3, Amelia and Opal were prepared to do what was required of them if necessary.

Arnold Paul was the baby of the crew; he was only twenty-seven when Voyager 3 took flight and was often the butt of most of Hugh's jokes.

"Is the ink dry on your degree?" Hugh would ask.

The first time Hugh said this, Arnold responded with a grin, "Yeah, old man. The degree came in the mail four years ago."

The third and fourth time, Arnold simply smiled sardonically at the comment. By the hundredth time, it was clear that Hugh wasn't getting the memo that the joke wasn't funny anymore, and by the thousandth time Hugh said it, Arnold simply stopped hearing him.

Arnold's youth played to his favor though. He was the only one to actually hold a graduate degree in aerospace engineering, a relatively new field of study. Though there were aeronautical engineering programs available prior to Arnold's schooling, he was among the first class of aerospace engineering graduate students. His knowledge of spacecraft and space travel in general was invaluable in the event of any necessary repair to the Voyager 3, or if adjustments had to be made to their flight path. Arnold was also a math wizard and frequently could be found calculating and re-calculating trajectories or trying to find opportunities for gravitational assists from celestial bodies.

Despite his tendency towards the analytic, Arnold was an avid patron of the theatre, lover of literature, and his favorite films were romantic comedies. He saw *Annie Hall* when it was released in April of 1977, but sadly he missed out on many romcoms from the rest of 1977 and later. Though he never saw the Travolta film version of Grease released in June of 1978, Arnold had played the part of Roger (replaced by Putzie in the film version) in a school production and had seen a professional production of the musical in Chicago in 1971. He was apt to burst into song on occasion—particularly "Rock 'n Roll Queen" as that was one of his numbers in the musical. More often, Arnold would quote lines from films he loved, mostly from *Harold and Maude, Play it Again, Sam, What's up,*

Doc?, The Apartment, Breakfast at Tiffany's, That Touch of Mink, and particularly from his favorite, Kiss Me Stupid.

"I have an amazing mother, you know. She's eighty-five and she don't need no glasses. She drinks right out of the bottle," was one of his favorite lines, and he used it whenever he could get away with it. Or, "if it weren't for Venetian blinds, it'd be curtains for us…" Or, "I need another song like a giraffe needs a strep throat."

The other three members of the crew weren't sure what to make of Arnold's love for that film, as none of them had seen it and now had no way to see it, but Arnold did his best to recreate it for them.

Opal Watts was the secret weapon of the team. Her Navy background often put her at odds with Hugh (sometimes jokingly and other times more seriously), but her double-major in engineering and medicine, and then a graduate degree in biology, made her the utility player. She wasn't captain, but she could have been if that decision hadn't been made by seniority and sexism. Hugh was quick to denigrate her piloting in the Navy, but this was based on nothing other than his own egotism. The truth was, Opal was top of her class and familiar with helicopters and planes. She was consulted by Rockwell when it was creating the plans for the XFV-12, and Opal likely would have been one of the first to pilot it if she hadn't made her decision to participate in the Voyager 3 program.

Despite her obvious competency as a pilot, Opal ultimately was selected for the team because of her work with genetic engineering. She had done her graduate work at University of Illinois and was part of the Illinois Long-term Selection Experiment. While that work was related to corn, Opal saw the implications for other genetic selection. As a result, she was designated the "broth cook" of the reproduction team, while Amelia was the one to actually handle the procedure.

Every team member had a say in the books, music, and entertainment brought on board, but Opal led the charge for music education. In the debate over the 8-track verses the humble cassette, Opal came down squarely on the side of the cassette. She preferred vinyl to either and, while she appreciated the innovation to skip directly to another track that the 8-track provided, she never really found the need to skip tracks because she only owned albums that she loved in their entirety. Therefore, the seamless play of the cassette won out. In the end it didn't matter so much what she preferred because an 8-track player and its cartridges would have taken up significantly more room than the cassette player and its cassettes. The team had already eliminated 8-tracks as an option before Opal officially made her position known.

The crew was each limited in the number of cassettes they could take, which gave Opal hours of agony deciding which albums were essential to the foundation of a new generation of human beings. She finally settled on The Beatles, The Rolling Stones, Ray Charles, The Supremes, and The Zombies. She also included one of her favorite musicians, Walter Carlos. She had to dub her records onto cassette to make them fit, but she brought *Switched-On Bach*, the soundtrack to *A Clockwork Orange*, and Opal's personal favorite, *Sonic Seasonings*. There was just something about the way that Carlos blended classical compositions with modern synthesizers that Opal loved. She could listen to the four sides of *Sonic Seasonings*—each named for a season—over and over and over again.

Opal wasn't on Earth to learn of Walter's transition to Wendy Carlos, or to read the interview that Wendy gave of the operation in *Playboy* in 1979, but even if Opal had known, she wouldn't have cared because Wendy continued to make the same ground-breaking music.

Once on board, Hugh, Amelia, Arnold, and Opal cross-taught one another all the skills they knew. In part, they did this out of necessity but also because they had nothing else to do. They read books, listened to music, jotted notes in their journals, and told stories.

"What else are we going to do for the 40,000 years it will take us to get where we're going?" asked Hugh, when Opal grew tired of Hugh's stories.

"Well, for starters, you won't make it to 40,000 years," Opal retorted.

"The hell I won't," said Hugh. "I've got good genes."

"There will be," Amelia rounded quickly and ran the numbers in her head, one thousand, two hundred generations between you and the people who finally find their way to the Alpha Centauri system." She paused and then added, "Give or take, depending on what a generation ends up looking like on board here."

"Even the best genes aren't going to extend your life that far, buddy," said Arnold.

"Amelia makes a good point; we're counting a human generation to be based on, depending on who you ask, twenty-five to thirty-three years, but generations on this ship might stretch longer than that."

Initially, the original crew members enjoyed the opportunity to tell one another stories and to have a captive audience with nothing better to do than to listen. Eventually, when Kirk, and then Rebecca and Sidney were born and finally old enough to understand the stories told to them, it was a huge relief to the original crew who had grown tired of hearing one another's stories. With the new crew members, and each successive generation, they took turns telling stories so the older members wouldn't have to suffer through repeated tellings of the same tired tales.

Notably, the original crew members had one important thing in common that the new humans would never experience: a lived life on Earth. Maybe they weren't born in the same towns, or knew the same people, but Earth-bound experience at least gave them a common understanding. Each new generation born in space didn't have that. Not only was their bone density less than the original crew members, but the newer generations had no concept of what any of the references to Earth, or life on Earth, meant. They were completely reliant on the original crew members to fill in all those gaps.

3—ANNOTATED NOTES TAKEN FROM THE HANDWRITTEN JOURNALS OF HUGH, VOYAGER 3

I always wanted to be an astronaut. As a kid, I tried to learn everything I could about space. I read every Burroughs's novel I could get my hands on. I wasn't as fascinated by his Tarzan books, though I read some of those too, but I consumed his Mars books, and I think all of the Venus ones as well. Burroughs called it the *Barsoom* series. If we had more room, I would have brought all ten or eleven, or however many of those books there were. The *Moon Men* book wasn't all that great, and neither were those *Caspack* books. But, man, the Mars and Venus series. As a kid, I can't even tell you how many times I read those books. Then there were the comics. Like, *Space Worlds, and Strange Worlds, and Space Adventures*, and *Strange Adventures*. Some of those were Timely, which became Atlas, and finally turned into Marvel. You know, Stan Lee, Spiderman, Iron Man, and so on.

"What's a comic?" asked Kirk. *There were always a number of words that the mission-born kids didn't understand. Kirk wasn't sure what a Tarzan was, or Barsoom, or Caspack.*

It depends. See, there are comic strips, which are usually goofy, silly things. Like *Peanuts, or Dennis the Menace*, or, uh,

Blondie. Wait, those names don't mean anything to you. Sorry. Okay, imagine a short story told in pictures. The cartoonists, the people who draw the comics, don't try to render people life-like; they make them as caricatures of real people.

"Caricatures?" asked Sidney. *Sidney often found herself stumbling over a word. It would sound familiar, and yet it was awkward on her tongue. She liked new words and their meanings. Sidney wondered aloud if "caricatures" might be a German word, but she was only basing that on her idea that German sounded harsh.*

Anyway, a caricature. A silly likeness. They would exaggerate the size of someone's nose, or make their eyes really expressive. Here, like this. See how this kind of looks like you, only your hair is much bigger and your eyes aren't really this big?

"Why would they draw people like that?" asked Sidney. *Paper was a limited resource on Voyager 3, and so it made sense that she wondered why someone would waste paper on a silly likeness. And yet, despite that, she asked for one to be drawn for her so she could see it for herself instead of just imaging it.*

To be funny? I don't know, honestly. But, usually the characters would do something silly, or get in trouble, or make fun of something that was really going on in the world. But a comic strip was maybe three or four panels long.

"How big was a panel?" asked Kirk. *Kirk was frustrated that we hadn't brought one of these comics with them so they could just look at one. If it was important, and it must be important because we were talking about them, then he should be able to see one for himself and be able to draw his own conclusions about them.*

It depended. In a newspaper, there might be dozens of comic strips, and so cartoonists didn't have much room. Maybe each panel was an inch square? They weren't like fine art or anything; each image would be detailed enough to give you a sense of what was going on, so you could get the joke.

"What kind of jokes did they have?" asked Sidney. Sidney usually struggled to understand the jokes the older crew told. *Often Opal or Arnold—the two who liked to joke the most—had to explain the background and context in order to understand the punchline.*

Sidney usually could understand the twist, or surprise or the play on words, but it rarely made her laugh.

A reoccurring joke in Peanuts was that Lucy would hold a football for Charlie Brown to kick it, and before he had a chance to connect with the ball, she'd pull the football away, and he'd land on his back.

"Why would she do that?" asked Kirk. *To Kirk, it seemed like a fairly mean thing to do, and Kirk was somewhat appalled that people might think it was funny.*

Because she was mean, and it was funny.

"What's funny about someone getting hurt?" asked Rebecca. *Rebecca had cut herself before, and didn't see anything funny about it. Maybe if she understood what a football was, maybe it was a different kind of hurt?*

Generally, people thought it was funny if someone else got hurt, as long as it wasn't someone they loved or as long as that person wasn't seriously hurt. Plus, the reader knew it was coming, but Charlie Brown always believed that his friend would hold the football for him. He'd ask, "And you're not going to pull it away are you?" and Lucy would always say that she wouldn't, but at the last moment, she'd pull the football away and he'd fall. Every time.

"That just seems mean," said Rebecca.

"What's a football?" asked Kirk. *Kirk, like Rebecca, was convinced that knowing what a football was might be central to understanding the joke.*

It's an oblong ball used in a sport. Don't worry about it. Back to comics. So, you had the comic strip, which we just talked about, and then sometimes there were comic books. These started out as books that collected the comic strips, so you could read them all in one place. But, then someone started writing stories for the books. So, I would read Space Squadron, and it would have three different stories in there. Each would be like 10 pages long, and then there'd be some ads and that kind of thing. They'd cost ten cents, or sometimes a quarter.

"What's an ad?" asked Rebecca. *She knew better than to*

interrupt, but she couldn't help it. The stories were long, and if she waited until he was done telling it, she often forgot her questions. Sometimes she could understand a word from the context, but other times she couldn't. She'd never heard the word "ad" before.

Well, that's short for advertisement. It's an image, or a short piece of text, that tries to convince you to buy something. Sometimes they are selling books, or gimmicky things like cheap toys, or live animals. I remember ordering the Krak-a-Jap machine gun from my older brother's old War Victory Comic. But, that book had come out in 1943, and by the time I got around to saving up the couple of bucks to buy it, the company had gone out of business. Thankfully the post office sent my letter back to me with my two dollars inside it.

"What's a machine gun?" asked Sidney. *Sidney knew the word machine, but she hadn't encountered gun before, and definitely hadn't heard machine and gun put together like this. She figured it must be some kind of automated thing, or maybe it was a programmable thing.*

"Who was your older brother?" asked Kirk. *Hugh often told stories about his childhood or his adult life, but he rarely mentioned anyone in his family.*

"What kind of animals could you get in the mail?" interjected Rebecca. *Amelia had explained the mail to Rebecca a while ago, but Amelia hadn't mentioned that you could send animals through it.*

I never tried to order any of the animals, but there were supposed to be some sea creatures, and a fish, and someone said there was even a monkey you could buy. But, like I said, I really didn't try that, so I don't know if they really shipped you anything. Sidney, a machine gun is an automatic gun. A gun is a weapon that fires bullets, which are propelled by gunpowder. We don't have any guns, or gunpowder on this craft. But, suffice it to say, guns are used for killing things and for war. Kirk, my older brother's name was Marco.

"What does it mean for someone to be your brother?" asked Sidney. *Sidney had heard about brothers and sisters and mothers and fathers before, but she wasn't really sure she understood how that all worked. The kids were ten, but there wasn't any reason to have explained any of this to them before.*

It means we share the same parents. If you only share one of the same parents, then any other child that parent might have become your half-brother or half-sister.

"Are these my sisters?" asked Kirk. *Kirk had read all about brothers and sisters, but he had never stopped to ask if he had any, and how Sidney and Rebecca were related to him (if they were).*

In a way, but not really. You all come from different genetic material, so you don't really share mothers. Technically, Kirk and Sidney, Amelia gave birth to both of you, which would usually mean you were brother and sister. But, since we implanted an egg of different women and used sperm from different donors, you share no maternal link. And, Rebecca, the same goes for you, except that Opal gave birth to you. Anyway, where was I going with this?

"You started telling us about always wanting to be an astronaut," said Rebecca.

"And then you told us about books and comic books," said Sidney.

Right. Well, back then, we hadn't had anyone in space, so we didn't know what it was like. But writers, like Burroughs and the people writing for the comics, they tried to imagine what it was like.

"Did they get it right?" asked Sidney.

No, not really. So far, I haven't met any Martians. And I haven't seen any UFOs.

"What's a UFO?" asked Kirk.

An unidentified flying object. We always thought space aliens would have some kind flying saucer, but I haven't seen anything like that yet. In the comics, people like Rusty Blake were always battling aliens on Mercury, or spacemen were flying to Mars and harvesting resources to bring back to Earth. But by the time I left, we had only ever made it to the moon. It was neat, but we didn't really find anything. Just some space rocks, and that astronauts who made it there got to jump around in the limited gravity.

"Do you miss Earth?" asked Rebecca.

Sometimes. But, my brother Marco is dead, and so are my parents. And, honestly, I didn't have very many friends. I put all my eggs in this basket.

"What does that mean?" asked Kirk. *Kirk found these idioms difficult to follow. He understood the words being used—eggs and basket—and knew that you could put eggs in a basket, but he didn't understand what that had to do with the story Hugh was telling.*

I just mean, everything I did was so that I could become an astronaut. That meant a lot of training, and education, and practice, and being ready if they ever called. It didn't leave a lot of time for friends or relationships. There was no plan B or back-up plan for me. It was being an astronaut or bust. I mean, I had a newspaper route when I was young and worked a few odd jobs before getting into school, but nothing that I would have done for the rest of my life.

"What other kind of jobs are there on Earth?" asked Sidney. *Sidney had never considered the possibility of having a different job. As far as she knew, there were just two jobs on the space ship— astronaut and genetic engineer—and she was both. They all were. Sidney wondered if there were other options on Voyager, or if there'd be more options when they got to Alpha Centauri. If there were other options, why was she just learning about these options now?*

All kinds of jobs.

"How does someone decide what they want to do? How do they get to choose? Does someone help them decide?" asked Rebecca.

It depends. Sometimes people take one job because it pays better than another one, or maybe they take a job because it's all they're capable of. Other people go to school a long time in order to get enough training for a particular job. Like Opal, Amelia, Arnold, and me. We had a lot of school to learn the things we needed to know in order to do this mission.

"But, that doesn't answer my question about what types of jobs there are on Earth," said Sidney.

People work in factories, or at gas stations, or grocery stores, or department stores, banks, and all kinds of things. They run businesses, or write books, or create advertisements.

"What's a factory? Or gas station? Or grocery store?" asked Kirk.

Oh boy. This might take a while.

4—TAKEN FROM THE AUDIO CASSETTE RECORDINGS OF OPAL, VOYAGER 3

From Tape #7a:

Just listen. I know you have questions but hold them. This is important. It isn't like Hugh's stories, which are always about himself. That man wants to live forever; he wants to be remembered. But this is about human beings and how resilient we are. This is about who you are, where you come from, and how we got to where we are now. So, listen.

On Earth, there are lots of living creatures, and there have been even more that have gone extinct for various reasons. But humans, you and me and everyone like us, have risen above everything else. There's nothing on Earth we can't conquer or kill or master. We rule the planet. That can be a good thing, because we don't have to worry about much or look over our shoulders for some hungry creature that might want to eat us. There are animals that can kill humans, like bears, tigers, lions, and sharks. Don't worry about what they are, just know they can best a human that's unprepared. If a human is ready, the human will come out on top.

We've found cures for diseases and for physical limitations. We've overcome blindness and created artificial limbs for people born without them. Occasionally, there is a war, which is basically when two groups of people don't get along and try to settle their differences by killing one another. For the most part, we get along. We find a way to communicate with people in countries that speak different languages from us. We invented phones to speak across great distances and computers that can calculate great sums quickly. There are other species that communicate with one another, and there are ones that work cooperatively, and others that help injured or weaker members of their species, but humans take this to a level that no other species on Earth does. That's you; that's us.

Then we calculated how to leave our planet.

Of all our accomplishments, that has to be the thing I'm most proud of. First, we sent people to our moon—which is like a small planet that orbits Earth. Next, we launched two probes, Voyager 1 and Voyager 2, deep into space to communicate back with Earth and send images of things we can't see from earth. And then, finally, we managed to create this craft you're on, our most impressive humble home we call Voyager 3. It's a little cramped at times, and you might want more privacy than you have, but take a second and truly marvel at how self-sufficient and contained it is.

We figured out how to reuse waste and turn it into drinking water and food. You can thank food scientists for figuring out how to use microbes to transform human waste into protein-rich food. We currently use freeze-dried food to help mix it up, but eventually that will be gone, and we will be completely sustained by a perpetual system.

You should be proud to be a human. In the short time between the designing of Voyager 1 and Voyager 3, scientists managed to double its velocity. This meant that while Voyager 2 launched first, Voyager 3 passed it like it was standing still. It will take Voyager 1 eighty-five thousand years to get to the Alpha Centauri System, but we'll get there in half that time.

Forty-some thousand years is a long time. Absolutely. But, considering we have a billion years before our sun starts boiling the Earth, and four billion before the sun fully absorbs the first four or five planets of our solar system and ultimately explodes, forty-thousand years is a drop in the bucket, and our sacrifices are small compared to the payoff of being able to provide answers and opportunity for the future of humanity.

Hugh's stories might be fun to hear, and it might be novel to learn about things from Earth, but, ultimately, that shit doesn't matter. This does. The legacy of humanity needs to be passed down from generation to generation.

One thing Opal didn't mention in her conversations with the new crew was race and how people on Earth dealt with superficial differences between one another. Such a small team needed to bond and unite, not divide and differentiate. Why give them tools to speak of difference if unnecessary? The original crew knew it pained her, because she foresaw a future when race would become an issue, and they wouldn't be prepared to deal with it. Opal didn't want anyone to face the challenges she had as a child, and this was one of the few topics that Opal had felt strongly enough to voice her opposition to the original crew.

From Tape 1b:

None of them realize how damaging their attitudes about race can be. It is downright frustrating to get into these conversations with them.

"Look, none of you realize the damage it can do," I said.

"Opal, that's offensive," said Arnold. "Just because I'm not black, doesn't mean I can't speak intelligently about slavery and Jim Crow and segregation and all that."

"I'm glad you took your history lessons seriously," I retorted. "But, there's so much more at stake than that. We have an opportunity here for a clean slate. A fresh start."

"Oh please," said Hugh. "If there's one iota of difference, someone will notice it and use it to their advantage. It's just the way we're built." Hugh knew I didn't appreciate this opinion, but he carried on anyway. "I realize, I'm a white male and all that, so what do I know? But I was a fat kid at one point. And I wasn't the type of fat who was big and could be intimidating. That just wasn't me." He paused uncomfortably, and thankfully the rest of the crew looked him skeptically. "I grew out of it. But the point is, because I was different people made fun of me and treated me different."

"I don't think anyone's getting fat on the diet we have on board here," Amelia replied. I know she was trying to lighten the mood, but part of her was being serious. How could anyone get fat on this food? "But I understand your point. Kids can be cruel. I think the difference is, here we have a unique opportunity. Like Opal said. But, more than that, the group is so small, there isn't an opportunity for some to gang up on another."

"I disagree," I quickly interjected. "I always faced the most discrimination in small groups. It didn't have to be a mob; it just took two people to team up. And that can definitely happen on here."

"Hasn't happened so far," said Arnold dismissively. "I mean, I know baby Kirk isn't going to team up with anyone, but I'm talking about us. I don't think any of us have paired up or teamed up against anyone else. Have we?"

He had a good point. Unlike my argument against discussing differences, we had all experienced racial differences on Earth. Yet, on board we've managed to work together and treat each other with respect. At least so far.

But, as usual, I couldn't help myself. "As the only black woman," I calmly restated, paused, and then restarted, "as the only black person on this ship, I feel very strongly that we don't talk about race. Let's see what happens. We're bound to have other racial differences in the sperm and eggs on board, right?"

Of course, we don't know that. Most of the NASA employees are white, but none of the team did the reproductive material collection, so it is possible. I'm hopeful.

Then Hugh surprised me by actually agreeing with me!

"I guess I'm on board," he said. "If it comes up, we'll address it. But, if it doesn't, let's leave it out of the education component."

"No reason to put ideas in their heads," said Arnold quickly added.

Eventually Amelia agreed, too.

So now I have taken ownership of the "history of humanity" lessons for the new generations. This frees everyone else up to focus on things that they think are more important. Arnold is pretty convinced that the version of humans that eventually reach the Alpha Centauri System, assuming they reach it, will bear little resemblance with the Earthbound humans anyway, making the "history of humanity" completely unnecessary.

Indeed, as Amelia predicted, each successive generation felt less and less of an attachment to Earth and instead felt more and more connected to the Voyager 3 and its mission. Unfortunately, the original crew couldn't answer very many questions about the Alpha Centauri System, other than to say, "It's the nearest sun-sized solar system like ours, and we believe there may be a planet or two that could sustain life." It was a completely honest answer, but it did little to inspire the crew that was born on the ship.

5—EARTH: VOYAGER 4, LAUNCHED MAY 2001

Every attempt was made to keep the launch of Voyager 4 secret on May 30, 2001. The launch was not announced, and no official statement was issued. Each of the other STS—Atlantis, Discovery, and Endeavour—had already had highly publicized and successful missions that year on February 7, March 8, and April 19, and NASA was anticipating successful launches for July 12, August 8, and December 5.

Despite their best efforts to launch Voyager 4 under the radar, so to speak, they knew there were simply too many eyes and ears to achieve the level of secrecy that had been reached in 1977 with Voyager 3. It was decided that if anyone asked, NASA would confirm an unofficial STS launch had taken place and deflect further questions. If this was met with persistence, then the official response would be, "You'll have to file an FOIA request to obtain more information about that matter."

Surprisingly, after the secret launch, no inquiries were made, and no FOIA requests were filed. It helped that public interest in the space program had waned, and its budget reflected that disinterest. In 1966, NASA's budget was at an all-time high, making up 4.41% of the Federal Budget—the equivalent of 43,554 million dollars (or 5,933 million dollars in 1966-dollars). By 2001, the budget was 0.76% of the Federal Budget. The last time NASA's budget was at 1% of the Federal Budget was back in 1993. In 1965 the organization had 41,100 in-house employees and over 300,000 contractors working for it. Since the mid-90's, NASA had been hemorrhaging 500 employees every year, and by 2001 there were only 18,872 in-house employees and 15,000 contractors remaining on its payroll.

NASA worked hard to make 2001 a banner year, scheduling a record of 18 spacewalks—12 from shuttles and six from the space station. People just weren't that interested. Instead, viewers watched the Baltimore Ravens beat up on the New York Giants in Super Bowl XXXV, and invested time in weekly television shows. By the time Voyager 4 launched, the top three programs had already aired their season finales. *CSI: Crime Scene Investigation* debuted to strong ratings, and its season finale featured a stymied attempt to track a serial killer. The *Friends* season seven finale was a double-episode featuring the wedding between Monica and Chandler, but it was really the *ER* season seven finale that captured people's attention.

The episode featured Derek Fossen (played by Ted Marcoux), an angry parent whose child had died in the previous episode. Fossen lashed out by killing seven people and injuring dozens of others before being shot and brought into the ER where Dr. Mark Greene was on duty. On his way to the operating room for surgery, Fossen had a heart attack. Greene prepared the defibrillator, but, rather than using it to restart Fossen's heart, Greene discharged it in the air and let Fossen die.

It was an intense episode and the discussions over the water color the following morning, often went something like:
"Wow."
"*ER*?"
"Yeah. That was pretty fucked up."
"Wait, what was?"

"That Dr. Greene killed him."

"But he killed all those people."

"I know. But doctors are supposed to save people, not make judgements like that."

"That poor father."

"He was an abusive father!"

"I don't think so. I think we're supposed to jump to that conclusion, like Greene does, but I think the father was just as surprised by the abuse as anyone else."

"Still, you don't get to shoot that many people and then have your life saved."

And so on. It was an episode that divided friends and continued to spark discussions almost two weeks later.

After the conclusion of the regular television season, people turned in to the NHL and NBA playoffs and finals. The NHL Stanley Cup came first, with a seven-game series between the Colorado Avalanche and the New Jersey Devils. It was close, but the Avalanche won and the team's goalie, Patrick Roy, was declared the MVP of the series. As the ice rinks were being shuttered for the season on June 9, the NBA playoffs neared their conclusion. Initially, it looked like the Philadelphia 76ers had a chance to make a run at the Los Angeles Lakers when Allen Iverson scored 48 in the opening game, beating the Lakers 107-101 in overtime. But then LA shut the 76ers down and won the next four games. The MVP went to Shaquille O'Neil, but it could have just as easily gone to Kobe Bryant, Rick Fox, Derek Fisher, Horace Grant, or Robert Horry. The Lakers had a killer line-up that year and had just won back-to-back championships. To no one's surprise, they'd win it all the next year, too, becoming only the fifth NBA team to do so (joining the 1952-1954 Minneapolis Lakers, 1959-1966 Boston Celtics, 1991-1993 Chicago Bulls, and 1996-1998 Chicago Bulls).

Space exploration was the last thing on most American's minds in 2001. The attention of Americans was on their own pocketbooks, bank accounts, mortgages, and jobs. The global economy was in a serious slowdown that even George Bush's "largest tax cut in 20 years" couldn't solve. Even Janet Jackson's "All For You" summer jam struggled to lift spirits.

Two other major world events ended up helping bury the launch of Voyager 4 for good. First, tropical storm Allison became the costliest tropical storm never to reach full hurricane strength. Most of its impact affected Texas, but the Gulf Coast area in general suffered greatly. In addition to being destructive, its duration was unusual for a tropical storm. It began on June 4 and didn't end until sixteen days later. That's not long for a cyclone or typhoon—which can last a full month—but for a tropical storm never reaching hurricane-strength, in the southeast United States, sixteen days was abnormal.

The storm and its destruction drew a lot of the media's attention. In fact, the whole hurricane season of 2001 was regularly in the news. The 2001 season produced four major hurricanes, nine named-hurricanes, and seventeen storms in total. One of the named-storms, Erin, formed on September 1 and looked like it was tracking to hit New York City. Rain, winds, and severe thunderstorms rocked New York City all day on September 10, but by the morning of the 11th, it was clear the Hurricane Erin had veered east.

Tuesday, September 11, 2001, was setting up to be a beautiful day with clear skies, a high expected in the mid-70s, and light winds. Then two planes crashed into the Twin Towers.

Nearly every American sat glued to their television after the attacks on the Twin Towers, and Troy, Rose, and Harper were no exception. Rose went to Harper's school and checked her out after the second plane hit. She knew, as she was waiting in line with other parents to take their students out of school, that her fear was probably irrational. Planes being used to attack New York City and Washington, D.C. didn't mean anyone would attack Florida. The whole thing was so surreal; she didn't know what was likely, or rational, or to be expected. She just knew that she wanted her daughter home. She wanted to be able to hold Harper and know that she was safe.

When Harper came to the office, she was somber and quiet. Rose wondered what she knew, or what the school had told her, but they didn't speak. After a quick hug, they walked quietly to the car. Every channel on the radio was suddenly "talk radio" and yet no one seemed to really have anything to say. They all said, "We don't know what to say," which was how Rose felt.

Finally, she turned off the radio and asked, "So, what did they say at school?"

"A plane was used like a bomb," Harper said flatly. She was sixteen, but her answer sounded like something a younger child would say. The attack had that effect on people. Rose wasn't sure she could have described it any more succinctly. As she watched the television, she noticed the news anchors struggled with words. They kept referring to it as a "bombing," which Rose thought wasn't quite right. Yes, the plane had exploded, but it was more of a crash than a bombing. The fuel in the plane had exploded like a bomb, but when Rose thought of a bombing, she thought of someone planting a bomb or firing a missile. It would take a while before the common language of this event settled down.

Troy was planted in front of the television when they got home. He looked up when they opened the door.

"Thank god," he said. "Mom's here. She's in the bathroom."

The three of them cuddled on the couch and stared at the television. Louise emerged from the hallway and joined them in the living room but took up her perch on the recliner next to the sofa.

"Should we go somewhere?" Louise asked.

"Where would we go?" asked Troy.

Louise shrugged in answer.

A decade later, Troy and Rose were preparing for dinner. It was October 1, and their first grandchild was already nine months old. Harper and baby Grover were going to join them shortly. Ribs were on the grill, and coleslaw was waiting in the fridge.

"I heard this story on NPR this morning, about Dr. Harold Sonny White," Troy said while Rose placed napkins at the table settings, and Troy put out the silverware. "He was talking about his theory about how to make a functioning warp drive."

"Three names? I thought they reserved that kind of designation for serial killers and presidential assassins," Rose joked.

"Ha. Ha. Ha," Troy dragged out each "ha" before adding, "very funny."

"Sorry," said Rose. "A warp drive, like in Star Wars?"

"Yes! Can you imagine that? I guess his work is based on an idea this physicist Miguel Alcubierre had back in 1994, but it's only now starting to gain attention."

"Does he work for NASA?" asked Rose.

"Yes, and no," said Troy. "Alcubierre is from Mexico, and I know he worked in Germany for a while, at the place where Einstein worked. But, yes, Dr. Harold Sonny White is working at NASA for now."

"Wow. So, when is it going to happen?" Rose placed the final napkin.

"I hope in our life time. It would be amazing to see something like that happen. Dad would have loved it."

Troy was now thirteen years older than his father had been when he died, but not a day passed without Troy thinking about him. When a story like this caught his ear, he thought of his father more than usual. Lately, he'd been thinking a lot about him. What would dad make of it? Would he still be working at NASA? Grover, Sr. would have been sixty-seven. It's possible he would have continued working at NASA past the typical retirement age, particularly if there were projects like this one to keep his interest piqued. On the other hand, as much as Dad enjoyed his work, he had enjoyed his family more. He might have chosen retirement to spend as much time as possible with his children, grandchildren, and great grandchildren.

From down the hall, Troy heard the door open and his

daughter's voice, "Hey, we're here!" Harper plopped the diaper bag down on the floor and passed baby Grover to Rose's waiting arms.

"Careful, he's crawling and standing," Harper said. "It's only a matter of time before he's fully mobile. I just need to grab a few things from the car." And then she disappeared outside again before Troy could ask if he could help.

Baby Grover reached out and pinched his grandmother's nose and giggled as Rose blew air at him. "Got my nose!" Rose said, laughing right back at him.

The doorway framed this moment perfectly for Troy as he stood there watching his wife enjoy the moment all to herself. Seeing so much joy made him certain his father would have retired as soon as possible, regardless of whatever new technology might have been on the horizon. At least, that's what Troy was sure that he'd do.

Harper returned, and Grover's attention turned to her.

"What's this big boy going to be for his first Halloween?" Rose asked.

"Am I a terrible mother that I haven't given it any thought?" asked Harper.

"It's not like he's going to be walking door to door," said Rose. "But, our neighbors, you know Chuck and Tina, their granddaughter was this adorable pumpkin last year."

"Like the Anne Geddes photograph?"

"She's the one that puts babies in vegetables?" asked Troy, now joining them in the living room.

"Yes," Rose said to him. "No," she said to Harper. "Well, maybe it does look a little like that," she decided.

"There are still a couple weeks to go," said Troy. "Plenty of time."

"He could always be a little astronaut," said Rose.

"Aww," Harper said. "I like that idea. Just like his great grandfather."

"Well—" Troy started.

"We know, we know. He wasn't actually an astronaut, just a NASA scientist," said Rose. "But, come on. Your dad would have loved that."

"Just wrap him in aluminum foil," Troy joked. "Super cheap costume." He winked to make sure everyone laughed. In all seriousness, he didn't really think it was a terrible idea.

Despite the wink, his daughter sighed and said, "Daaaad." His wife rolled her eyes at him.

"You have twenty-nine days to decide. No pressure," Troy said. "I saw a cute peapod costume at Super Target yesterday." He felt better having put a more "serious" offer on the table. Both women nodded, and all eyes fixed on the baby. Grover smiled back and appeared to be very content. "Ribs should be done any minute now," Troy said.

"Your father seems to have forgotten everything he ever knew about raising children. He asked me earlier if Grover was going to be able to try some of his ribs."

Harper looked at her father. "Seriously, Dad? Maybe when he's two."

January 5, 2013, offered a special kind of resonance between the generations as they celebrated Grover's second birthday. Most obviously was how Baby Grover was playing with his mother's old childhood toys on the dusty attic floor. Harper remembered most of those toys fondly, and seeing her son play with them touched her in a way that sincerely surprised her. Troy and Rose were moved by seeing their grandson play with their daughter's toys, but they were more moved by seeing their daughter so moved by it.

There was also an air of resonance between Grover Sr. and Grover Jr. It was the day the forgotten mystery of the second launch was remembered, and the day Troy, Rose, and Harper decided to pursue more information through the FOIA form. Today would be remembered as an important day.

But first, the family gathered for a little boy's second birthday. Grover had now reached the milestone where he was no longer referred to in terms of months. No one in the family gave this much thought; it was just something that happened. Another thing that just "happened" was that everyone began calling him Grover Junior, or simply Junior. He wasn't technically a junior. He didn't share the same middle name with his great grandfather, but that didn't stop his mother from calling him Junior. At two, he had little to say about this development, and by the time he was old enough to care, the nickname had stuck.

"Speaking of milestones, you two have one coming up," Harper said. She was never very good at being subtle. "Thirty years is something to celebrate."

"It's the pearl anniversary," Troy said. "Let's get some oysters, and we'll eat our way to finding some."

"No, I'm serious," said Harper. "What do you guys want to do for it? How do you want to mark the occasion? How do you want to celebrate?"

"This," Rose gestured at the gathered family, "is all I need."

A knock on the door interrupted the conversation, and Troy jumped up and hurried to answer it.

"Hello?" Louise cooed, as Troy opened the door for her. Louise handed her son two bags of presents and stepped into the house. She quickly glanced around until she found Junior, locked eyes with him, and got down on the floor and crawled toward him.

"Hell-loooo," she said in a sing-song voice.

Junior was still young enough, he didn't seem to know what to make of this lady. He thought it was funny that she was on the floor. He certainly didn't crawl anymore, and it was weird seeing someone so much older than him doing it. This must be some game. Junior laughed and got down and crawled until the two of them bumped foreheads, and they laughed some more.

Louise was very active and engaged and was often mistaken for years younger than she actually was. People often mistook Troy for her brother instead of her son, and they sincerely had a hard time believing that she could possibly be this man's mother. All this worked in Grover Junior's favor, because, while his father was no longer in the picture, he had at least four loving adults who doted on him.

After the ribs were devoured, the gifts opened, the candles

blown out, the cake eaten, and the birthday boy put to bed, the adults sat in the living room talking.

"We were up in the attic earlier and guess what we found?" asked Troy.

"Apparently all Harper's old toys," said Louise, looking at the pile of dusty toys waiting to go home with Harper.

"Yes, but we also found that old box of Dad's papers and things." Troy waited to see how his mother would react, but she just smiled waiting for him to say more. "Remember how he had that folder, and I tried tracking down people on his lists?"

"Yes?"

"Well, Harper suggested that we file a Freedom of Information Act request, to see if we can find out anything else. What do you think?"

"Sounds interesting to me."

"Probably, we won't find anything," said Harper.

"But, you never know," added Rose.

"That could be exciting," said Louise. "Who knows!"

Troy filed the FOIA request, and then waited the allotted twenty days. He received a formal written response indicating that they would need more time to investigate the matter. He waited again and received another response two weeks later. The response indicated that there were some "irregularities" with the documents, and they needed still more time to conduct the research.

In the meantime, President Obama was officially sworn in as the 44th president of the United States. Various states approved same-sex marriage laws. Kirk, on board Voyager 3, chose to end his life. Pope Francis became the first pope selected from Latin America. George Zimmerman was acquitted of all charges in the fatal shooting of Trayvon Martin. The city of Detroit filed for Chapter 9 bankruptcy. And then finally, Troy received an envelope containing a letter and two documents on NASA letterhead.

The letter had a sticky note with a first name and a phone

number on it. Since neither of the documents made much sense to him, and the typed letter appeared to simply announce the investigation was at its end, Troy called the phone number.

"Hello?"

"Hello. I'm trying to reach Jackie King?"

"This is her."

"Jackie," Troy said. "I just received your response to my FOIA request and, honestly, I'm not sure what I'm looking at. Can you help me?"

"Of course, I'd be happy to help you with that. Can you please give me your name and the FOIA request number so I can pull that information up?"

"Right. I'm sorry. This is Troy Baines. The number is probably on these documents somewhere, but I—"

"Don't worry about the number, Mr. Baines. I know which file you're referring to." Jackie paused for a moment to collect her thoughts.

It was so quiet on the line Troy wasn't sure if she had hung-up. He was having a hard time reading her tone. Was she angry about the file and about his calling her? If so, why did she include her phone number? Finally, Jackie broke the silence.

"What you're looking at there are the only two documents that I could find regarding your request. One is a requisition for an abandoned prototype for the Gemini program—called the Big G. There's so little information on the form; it's hard to even really call it a requisition. The paperwork does acknowledge that modification work was being done on the Big G after the prototype had been shelved. The second document is a memo discussing weather conditions for the evening of the Voyager 2 launch."

"Huh," Troy said. So far Jackie hadn't offered anything new, other than simply summarizing the documents he had in front of him—like when a presenter reads each slide from the PowerPoint, or an instructor insists on reading the syllabus to the class.

"So, can you help me piece this together? How do these fit with my request regarding a secret third Voyager launch?"

"Officially, there is no third Voyager launch, Mr. Baines," Jackie said. "But, the two documents you hold seem to suggest that there was something going on with the old Big G, and someone was curious about flight conditions on the evening of the Voyager 2 launch."

"You know, I was a little boy in my backyard with a telescope that day. I watched Voyager 2 go up, and then I was still in the backyard later that day when I swore I saw something else go up. No one ever believed me."

"It's not often we get a FOIA request for something that turns out to be a possibility like this. Usually people are asking about Area 51, or to see documents related to aliens," Jackie said. "When I saw your request, I figured it was just another of those. But, I have to say, I think I kind of believe you."

"My father believed me," said Troy.

"Your father?"

"He worked at NASA, and he was digging around shortly before he died. I have some of his files, and I've been trying to make sense of them. I spoke to an ex-employee, and she said NASA harvested her eggs."

"Her eggs?" Jackie said. "You mean, as in, her reproductive material?"

"Yes. That's unusual, right?"

"Highly. Though they did a lot of strange experiments in the 70s. The whole Federal government did strange experiments back then. Who knows what they might have wanted them for . . ."

"What do I do from here?" Troy asked.

"Well, I've already escalated the request and will be handling the case myself. You've definitely piqued my interest."

This rather mundane conversation may not seem like the basis for a warm friendship that would last the rest of their lives, but it was just that. As a result of this chance happening—Troy's FOIA request landing in the lap of Jackie King, and Jackie King taking it seriously, and Jackie King leaving a sticky note with her personal phone number attached for Troy to reach out to, and Troy Baines actually taking the initiative to call her—the two formed a very close personal and professional relationship.

At first, their interactions were purely related to the FOIA request and the follow-up from Jackie's "escalation" of the matter. It wasn't long before they began bonding over a shared love of the stars and space in general, and before long, one or the other was being invited over for dinner with each other's families. As they found more and more in common with the other, they felt right at home with the rest of the family members.

Getting to the bottom of the secret Voyager 3 mission took nearly a year. Finally, thirty-seven years after the Voyager 3 took flight, the veil over the program was lifted entirely, and Jackie and Troy were able to interview two members of the small team that had kept it secret all that time.

Marc Sanders and Edmund Lawson were retired and nearing eighty, but they remembered quite clearly what had transpired. Yes, there was a secret manned flight on the evening of August 20, 1977. No, there really wasn't a massive cover-up so much as simply an omission and an intentional exclusion of the majority of the NASA team. At the time, artificial insemination and in vitro fertilization were fairly taboo, and it was decided that it would be easier to be forgiven than to have permission granted. Yes, everyone was handsomely compensated for the donation of their genetical materials. No, they weren't sure the project would work. Yes, they knew it was a big gamble. Yes, all the astronauts knew the risks they were taking, and they were willing participants. No one was coerced. Yes, they had lost contact with Voyager 3 almost immediately. Yes, they had told the parents of the astronauts that their children had died in 1977. No, they hadn't specified how or what had happened, and thankfully none of them had asked for more specifics. Yes, Grace Paul was one of the mothers they had spoken with. No, they really had no reason to assume anything bad had happened with the crew.

They simply had wanted to get ahead of whatever backlash might be coming, since they had no intention of sending another manned crew up there to try to retrieve them. Yes, we'd be happy to talk more if there were any other questions.

Marc Sanders and Edmund Lawson left, and Jackie and Troy sat in silence for a couple of moments.

"Well, what now?" asked Troy. It was gratifying to have some of his hunches and suspicions confirmed, and he really liked the idea that his father's DNA was somewhere in space looking down on him. Heck, he might even have a half-brother up there, navigating a spaceship. No, it wouldn't be a half-brother, because they wouldn't share a mother. What would that be? He wasn't sure what to call him, or her. Wow, he could have a sister!

"We publish," said Jackie. "This is a hell of a story."

The thought had never crossed Troy's mind. Once Jackie said it, it made a lot of sense. Other people would want to hear about it. Troy could write, but he had no idea where, or how, to publish such things.

"Where?" he asked.

"Any number of places. *Science*? *Advances in Space Research*? *Air & Space*? *Astronomy*? *Discover*? *Scientific America*?" Jackie said. "Or, heck, maybe even the New Yorker or New York Times or Atlantic Monthly."

It turned out, in addition to getting along well, they were excellent collaborators. Jackie took over most of the research and formalized writing parts, and Troy did the more narrative sections. This made sense as that part was his story to tell. The result was an engaging, well-researched essay that exposed what they had unearthed without defaming the space agency.

Voyager 3 was a failed experiment, everyone in the program had consented and knew what they were getting into, and sacrifices had to be made in order to advance the program. As far as NASA, Troy, and Jackie were concerned, Hugh Sullivan, Arnold Paul, Amelia Gardner, and Opal Watts were national heroes. *Discover* ran Troy and Jackie's story, and soon it was picked up and carried by other journals and papers. The public loved the story, and the four astronauts were granted a special memorial service, burial in Arlington, and a memorial statue was commissioned to honor them.

Eight years later, on December 17, 2022, Jackie was with the Baines family at the memorial to honor the 50th anniversary of the moon landing. The statue—simply titled Voyager—was on the Cape, but located a little out of the way. It was a convenient meeting place for their little celebration.

Junior was now eleven, and though he occasionally grumbled about being called Junior, he was grateful they'd stopped referring to him as Baby Grover. Harper was thirty-seven, Troy and Rose both fifty-seven, and Louise seventy seven. Recently, Jackie had started talking about retirement, which surprised Troy who often forgot she was six years older than him.

"But, there's one thing that might keep me going for a little while longer," Jackie said conspiratorially.

"Oh?" asked Rose suddenly curious. Over the years, she had come to think of Jackie as an honorary member of their family. "What's that?"

"You'll never believe it, but apparently there was a fourth Voyager launched in 2001."

"Manned?" asked Troy.

"Yep."

"You've got to be kidding me," said Rose. "How many of these are there?"

"Well, they didn't call it Voyager 4, because they didn't know about Voyager 3 at the time," said Jackie.

"And no one bothered to offer this up when we were working on our article?" asked Troy.

"Separate departments and decades separating them," said Jackie.

"And I guess, what with people flying planes into buildings," said Harper, "we were too distracted to notice."

"When did it happen?" asked Troy.

"Sounds like another article," said Rose. "Good for you two."

"You're practically the new Nellie Bly," said Louise.

"Who?" asked Troy.

"Ugh," Jackie punched him in the shoulder. "She exposed how terrible mental institutions were in the late 1800s. Don't you know anything about history?"

"I do, and I guess I even knew that. I was just caught off guard because my mother was suddenly comparing the two of us to a single reporter."

"What about Barlett and Steele?" asked Rose.

"Even better," said Louise. "I loved their work."

"While we," Jackie looked and nodded at her collaborator, "appreciate the compliment, I think we're a long way from a Pulitzer Prize-winning team like that."

"Right," said Troy. "What she said."

Far above them, millions of miles away, Voyager 4 passed Voyager 3 without so much as a second thought.

6 – SUICIDE IN SPACE, VOYAGER 3, 2013

The first suicide on board the Voyager 3 occurred in 2013. Kirk, now thirty-five, was the first child conceived on board and seemed to be receptive to the lessons he learned from his four adoptive parents. He eagerly listened and absorbed every morsel that Hugh, Arnold, Amelia, and Opal gave him. When they ran out of mission-related things, they taught him languages, though it was unlikely they would be useful on a foreign planet. Between the four original crew members, they knew seven languages, and before long Kirk was fluent in each of them. When additional children were born, the crew made an effort to educate everyone equally because they couldn't predict who would be the best teacher of future generations or more grimly, who would survive. Plus, since there was little else to do on board other than talk, that's what they did.

Hugh was the oldest crewmember at launch time had lived the longest on Earth, so he had more stories to tell. It also meant he was the last of the original crew to reach his space rebirth date. That's the name Opal came up with for the date at which your age in space exceeded your age on Earth. Hugh's was in 2013 when Voyager 3 reached the interstellar medium, which was further than any other Earth-made object had traveled. Voyager 1 and 2 wouldn't cross the heliopause until

2012 and 2018, and who knows how long until they found their way across the bow shock, let alone the interstellar medium, and that was assuming they kept keeping-on.

Maybe it was Hugh officially having passed more time in space than on Earth that prompted Kirk to end his life. Unlike Hugh, Kirk would never see Earth. He would never see the Alpha Centauri System either. His entire life would be encapsulated on this ship. He was merely a chink in the chain connecting Earth to Alpha Centauri.

Kirk had nothing original to offer to the next generation. All his stories were created from things he had heard someone else describe to him.

Nothing had driven this point home more than when Hugh said, "Well, now I'm reborn in space, and I'm younger than all of you. Of course, unlike you, I have a last name."

It was meant as a joke, and everyone had laughed, but as with much humor, it had a sharp edge of truth to it. Kirk, and the rest of the crew born on board, did not have last names. Amelia was Kirk's birth mother, but as protocol directed, her egg was not used. Had they realized the impact of needing a last name, they could have found the last names of the egg and sperm used to bestow a last name on Kirk. They could have simply created a last name. Amelia could have given Kirk her last name, as she had the strongest claim to him. Unfortunately, the original crew didn't see any reason to give him a last name. They didn't foresee a future where there would be enough people in Voyager 3 to need secondary names to tell one another apart.

None of them considered what would happen after the Voyager 3 completed its mission and established a colony. Perhaps they would eventually need a way of differentiating persons, but they'd have no knowledge of how people on Earth did it. Maybe they'd come up with a unique solution, like combining the first names of the parents to create a new name. Or, maybe they'd come up with using a second name, or a number, or perhaps, somehow, spontaneously, they'd create the very system that people on Earth had used.

When Kirk asked about why he didn't have a last name, Hugh shrugged and said, "You want a last name so bad? Give yourself one."

Kirk knew Hugh was right. He could give himself whatever name he pleased, but what was the point of that? Not having a last name was just one more thing that separated the new humans from the original crew, but giving himself a name wouldn't fix that. Kirk wondered what other traditions they might be forgetting to pass on. He'd never know. Outside of the books on board, he was subject to all his information being filtered through Hugh, Arnold, Amelia, and Opal.

The original four didn't have much else to do, but they grew tired of Kirk constantly asking for attention. He had read all the books on board. He even read the dictionary for fun, and spent time studying the origin of words. It was how he encountered the word "suicide" and learned it was coined in 1651; before it was "suicide," the situation was simply referred to as "voluntary death," or "self-homicide," or "self-murder." Similarly, Kirk learned that the word robot came from a Czech word that translated as "forced labor." He eagerly shared this information with the original crew members, but only Arnold seemed interested.

"I didn't know that," Arnold said.

"Does anyone know the Czech language?" asked Kirk.

"No, sorry; we're out of languages," Arnold said.

"Did you know that avocado comes from an Aztec word that means 'testicle'?"

"No," said Arnold. "Also, we don't know any Aztec languages, or have any avocados for you to try. Sorry."

"What do they taste like?"

"Well, they're green," started Arnold.

"Yes, green and pear-shaped. Tough outer skin and soft inside," said Kirk. "That's what I know about it. But, how do they taste?"

This kid, thought Arnold. He shook his head a little and then answered, "Well, they're kind of creamy. It depends if they're ripe or not. They can be hard, and they have a big pit in the middle of them."

Arnold remembered visiting his aunt in San Luis Obispo and picking an avocado right from the tree. "My aunt always said, check the sides of the avocado. It should squish a little, but not too much. Then she'd hold it in her hand and cut around it with a knife. Whack the pit with the knife and toss the pit into the trash. I always liked it fresh, with some salt and lime juice. So, I'd just score the meat with the knife, careful not to go all the way through, squeeze some lime over it, and sprinkle a little salt. Then I'd scoop it out with a spoon. It was delicious."

"But what did it taste like?" Kirk asked.

Arnold thought for a moment, and said, "Kind of buttery? Kind of nutty? It's weird; it doesn't have a strong flavor, but it was wonderful in combination with things. Most people probably think they've tried avocados, but they've only ever eaten guacamole. Which, don't get me wrong, is probably the best way to eat avocados, but the fruit is so buried under garlic and onion and lime, that you're not really tasting avocado."

"What does guacamole taste like?" asked Kirk.

It was a never-ending cycle with him. He'd come for one piece of information, and within the explanation he'd find six other questions to ask.

Hugh taught Kirk about decompression sickness and hypoxia. These were very real concerns if someone wanted to leave the craft and were included in the basic lessons taught to every new crew member. However, traveling at the speed they were, it was unlikely any of them would ever leave the shuttle, but the information needed to be passed on for when it would eventually matter.

Thus, this information had to be passed on. Just imagine if, in the 41,000 years it would take to arrive at the end of their mission, the Voyager 3 touched down and the crew, so far removed from the four that initially set out, went to leave the craft without taking the proper precautions. If their lives trapped on this vessel wasn't tragic enough, that ending would render useless all the sacrifices they, and everyone that was part of the legacy of Voyager 3 had made to make that moment possible.

It never occurred to Hugh that someone would use decompression sickness as a way to end their life intentionally. It wasn't the worst way to die, but there certainly were more peaceful ways to go. Then again, Hugh didn't see any reason someone would want to commit suicide.

"You know the bends?" Hugh had asked while teaching Kirk the basic survival skills of emerging from the shuttle.

He knew it was a stupid question the minute the words were out of his mouth. Kirk wouldn't know about the bends unless he had read about them in a book, or if one of the other crew members happened to have mentioned it.

"Sorry. Let me start over. Sometimes they call it the bends. But the real name is decompression sickness, or DCS. Basically, you need to adjust pressures carefully so everything matches. Don't rush it."

"Don't rush what?" asked Kirk.

Hugh realized he was doing a poor job of this. If the kid had ever gone diving, it would be easy to explain the necessity to ascend slow and steady. In this case, it was simply a matter of standing in a room and adjusting the pressure.

"Well, on board a spacecraft, it's best not to rush anything. My dad used to say measure twice and cut once. Do know understand what that might mean?"

"I guess; make sure of yourself?"

"Right. Same here. First, do things to protect yourself against it. Remain hydrated."

"What does water have to do with decompression?"

"Honestly, not sure," Hugh admitted. "I just know it helps. But, basically, just take my word for it. Stand in the airlock and wait until the meter hits its mark. Then it's safe to exit the module."

"What would happen if I didn't?" asked Kirk.

"That's where we come back to DCS."

"What happens if I never re-pressurized? Like if my suit

tore while I was outside, or something like that?"

"You'd die pretty quick," Hugh wasn't one to mince words. "Either from radiation exposure or from lack of oxygen. Suffice it to say, be careful not to let it happen."

Someday, when a future crew landed somewhere in the Alpha Centauri System, Hugh hoped they would be able to remove their suits and live in an environment without all this gear or worry about airlocks or depressurization. That was centuries away from Kirk's time, and Hugh honestly didn't know what that environment was going to be like, so there was no real way to prepare anyone for it.

It will happen when it happens, whatever it is, Hugh thought to himself.

The crew should have seen Kirk's suicide coming, but they didn't and were surprised when it happened. Kirk seemed like such a bright guy. In hindsight, which is always full of greater clarity, they saw signs of Kirk's discontent. Of all the books on board, Kirk's favorite was Goethe's *The Sorrows of Young Werther*.

As Amelia watched Kirk's body disappear from view, his head bare in the dark of space, she couldn't believe she hadn't put two and two together. She wasn't his birth mother in the traditional sense, but she did give birth to him. Didn't mothers feel some kind of innate connection to their child, and if so, why hadn't she? Why didn't her Spidey-sense tingle and tell her that something was wrong with Kirk? For God's sake, how had she missed it when Kirk had said, "Mom, this part, I don't understand" and then he read her a paragraph from *Werther* that describes the young protagonist's suicide and how, "a vein was opened in his right arm: the blood came, and he still continued to breathe."

Amelia had looked at him and matter-of-factly said, "Well, on Earth people decide to end their lives sometimes. It's called suicide. Sometimes they do it with a gun, or a knife."

"Werther used both," Kirk had interrupted impatiently.

"I guess he just wanted to make sure then," she had said.

Amelia didn't think more about it. Kirk was just ten then, and he probably gravitated to the book because it was so skinny. What was it, ninety pages? Amelia wasn't sure, but she was pretty convinced its inclusion on Voyager 3 was merely due to how little space it took up. The book became a bit of a fascination for Kirk, and provided an opportunity for Arnold to tell him how the book was originally written in German. This piece of information became the impetus for an exercise where Arnold challenged Kirk to translate it from the English back into German. When Kirk was done, Arnold wished they had a copy of the original 1774 to see how well Kirk had managed, but Arnold was pretty convinced he had done a good job.

Unlike Amelia and Hugh, when the light showed that someone was in the airlock, Arnold knew exactly what was happening. He understood. Being born into this was a lot. They had no choice in the matter. They were simply born and were immediately part of a mission. They were educated only to pass information onto the next group. They were nourished to continue the line of humanity until it reached the end of the mission. They had a built-in responsibility to reproduce via in vitro only to reduce the risk of genetic anomalies. Everything done on Voyager 3 was for the next generation. The crew didn't even have sex to look forward to for personal enjoyment. It was flatly restricted and regulated. Frankly, Arnold was surprised more of the crew hadn't already considered suicide.

Later, when everyone talked about their shock and surprise, Arnold was quiet. He was contemplating his own end on this craft. Kirk had only been thirty-five, but Arnold was sixty-three now. How much longer did he have? Regardless of when his end came, there would be an end of some kind. Even if the hypothesis was correct that humans, without Earth's gravitational fields, would live longer in space, there was no way Arnold was going to last forty thousand years. When he died, they would jettison him just as they had Kirk. They'd need his suit, and clothing, and everything else for the next generation. He'd be released out the airlock to tumble about in space, frozen and naked for all time. Hardly a comforting way to go.

Also, surprisingly, Arnold didn't object to the idea of killing himself. He was, at this point, just taking up space. He could reiterate lessons that he'd already taught the new batch umpteen times, but once they got it all down, it was their job to pass it on to the next generation. He had done his job. Occasionally, there were things he remembered that he hadn't told Kirk or Rebecca or Sidney or Eva, but those tidbits were so small, Arnold was convinced it wouldn't impact the mission. When Arnold talked to Hugh about feeling obsolete, Hugh's perspective was completely different.

"Haven't you ever played telephone?" Hugh asked.

"Of course."

"Well, then you know, just because you tell one person a thing, doesn't mean they can pass that on without altering it or misconstruing it."

"Sure, that's a game though. In this case, we have years with the new crew to make sure they have the information right before they have to pass it on," Arnold said.

"Check, doublecheck, and triple check," said Hugh. "Too much depends on this. If we're not here to ensure the quality and validity of the information, then this all could be for nothing. Imagine Kurt."

"Kirk," interrupted Arnold. "It's Kirk."

"Okay, doesn't change my point, but alright. Kirk passes it on to Amber and Amber passes it onto George. I know we don't have a George, I'm just making up names; please don't arrest me Mr. Name Police. And George passes it on, and so on for generations, and when the time comes, suddenly someone flips the wrong switch, or forgets how to use the airlock. There are disastrous consequences for not getting it right."

"But, that's always the case," said Arnold. "I see what you mean, but the simple fact is, we're not going to be there, hovering over their shoulders to make sure they do it right."

He paused and rubbed his eyes. "Besides, who's to say that we remembered it correctly anyway?"

Hugh laughed and that was the end of the conversation.

The biggest issue, the way Arnold saw it, was how to commit suicide without wasting limited resources or being a mess or nuisance for the rest of the crew. The way Kirk went was considerate to his crew because there was no clean up or corpse removal required. However, because he took a suit with him, the crew now had one less spacesuit. They had extras, but not enough if too many more people followed Kirk's example.

Someone would have said something if Kirk had abruptly stripped naked and headed to the airlock. And even if no one had noticed, what would he have done in the airlock? Just open the hatch? That would render the airlock chamber useless and dangerous for the next person. He could have depressurized the chamber and simply died there, but that would leave the mess for someone else to clean up.

Arnold abruptly interrupted his meandering thoughts as he realized that suicide was something they had to talk about.

"Look, with Kirk gone, others are going to follow his lead," Arnold said to the original crew in a closed-door session.

"Ridiculous. The boy was troubled," said Hugh. "No one else wants to die in space like that."

"It's reasonable to assume someone else will," said Opal. "At least one. Arnold's right; we need to be prepared."

Arnold talked through the issues he saw with suicide and the complications being on board a spaceship presented. "If someone wants to go, we need to help them."

"No way," said Hugh. "We need every life on this ship to make this mission successful."

"Not technically," said Opal. "We need a female and some of the sperm on board."

"Right," said Amelia. "But, if we were only going to have one person, a female, then we'd need that person to be young enough to reproduce, and to possess all the knowledge to make the mission a success."

"Good point. I guess really we need two, because we'd

need another to do the fertilization."

"You all are crazy," said Hugh. "We need a crew. A variety of perspectives and different sets of eyes to see what the others might miss."

"The women are talking about the extreme view, Hugh. You know that. Don't be so concrete," said Arnold. "The point is, not everyone is essential. Let's not deviate from my point. Some people are not going to like the idea of spending their entire lives in this little box hurtling through space."

"They didn't sign up for it; they've been forced into it," added Opal. "It's only natural that people, like Kirk, are going to want to opt out."

"Opt out," said Hugh. "How benign."

"You know what she means," said Amelia. "I think Arnold is right; we need to offer an opportunity to help those who want out. For any number of reasons, but most practically, as he pointed out, the loss of resources if they take matters into their own hands."

"And the potential mess if they try to do it on board, instead of outside," said Opal.

"I'm going to have to think about this a little more," said Hugh.

"What's there to think about? There are three in favor, and one on the fence," Opal said.

"I just don't like the idea of discussing suicide with the crew. What if we're putting the idea in their heads for the first time, and they never would have considered it otherwise?" said Hugh.

"The minute we talk about the inevitability of death, they're going to start realizing there's a way to shortcut the system," said Arnold. "And you know we have to talk about death, because that is something that will happen on board sooner or later."

"And, we have to talk about what happened with Kirk," said Amelia. "We have to explain why he isn't around all of a sudden."

Hugh didn't like it, but he had to admit to the logic of their argument. "Well, you three do the debriefing about Kirk and come up with a procedure for assisted suicide."

Though none of them would openly admit it, suicide actually performed a useful service on board. There weren't Earth-bound illnesses to contend with, and being away from the gravitational forces of Earth made the organs and body last longer, which meant the spaceship was quickly becoming crowded. The crew limited the reproductions as much as possible, and the original mission was to create a new generation every twenty-five to thirty years. This meant that they needed to have at least one female capable of reproducing, but even that wasn't so simple. It was hard to know whether or not that female was fertile or receptive to the fertilization techniques. Consequently, there was a push to have at least two females of reproductive age per generation.

All the original planning hadn't taken into account the fact that people would live longer and have fewer opportunities to do stupid things to get themselves killed. No one was falling into the Grand Canyon, or holding a firecracker too long, or cleaning a rifle. Simply put, death wasn't very present on Voyager 3. Suicide could help cull the ranks.

Hugh initially argued with Opal that it was essential to create a new generation with equal number to the original crew, but then saw the error of his ways when she pointed out the Voyager 3 was really only designed for nine to twelve. After several generations of new crew members, the ship was going to get crowded.

"But," argued Hugh, even though he knew he was losing the argument, "how do we know who will make it and who won't? Won't it compromise the mission to put all our eggs in one basket?"

"It's a risk we're going to have to take, or we're going to need to find a bigger ship."

Suicide helped maintain the balance.

When Kirk was born first, there was some relief that a baby could be born in space at all. There was no research to confirm their assumption of reproduction in space. That relief quickly turned to disappointment that Kirk was male. Had he been a female, it would have allowed the team to take a little more time before trying again. When Rebecca was born and then Sidney, Opal convinced Hugh that it was time to stop for awhile. They had two viable females.

Eva was the first born of the generation in the late-90s, then Edgar, and finally Amber. They had rushed to fertilize Amelia almost immediately upon leaving Earth because she had been thirty-one, and they weren't sure how many times it would take. When Kirk killed himself in 2013, Eva and Amber were only fifteen and fourteen, so there really was no rush. Opal was thinking they wouldn't even try until the girls were thirty-five, but in 2022, when the girls were in their early twenties, Hugh started making a fuss about it being time for a new generation. Opal countered that they could not afford to have more children until there was more room. Everyone knew what Opal was implying.

"Jesus," Hugh said to Opal. "What are you thinking?"

"She's just being very practical," said Arnold. "It's true. This thing was made for twelve astronauts, plus all our shit. It's not like we can expand it somehow."

"I'm sorry," said Opal. "They have the example of Kirk now, and we need to make sure only those that are the most committed to the mission go forward. We can't afford the space and effort on those that aren't fully invested."

"I'm surprised, Hugh, I mean, you seem so practically minded. Death seems to put you off balance," said Arnold.

"Suicide does, not death," Hugh said curtly.

"Just think about the mission's success," said Opal. "We have me and Amelia who are well past reproductive age, and Rebecca and Sidney are in their early forties now."

"I noticed you didn't mention Hugh or me," said Arnold. "It's okay to say it; we're both unnecessary, too. We've passed on our knowledge to the next generations, and we should step out."

"I'm not saying that," said Opal.

"But, you're not, not saying that either," said Hugh.

"All I'm saying is, very practically speaking here, we can't commit to reproducing more children until there is more room for human cargo," said Opal.

Amelia was the only original crew member not present for the conversation. She didn't need to be because she had already had a similar conversation with Opal. Though she hadn't felt particularly attached to Kirk in his life, somehow, since his passing, she had thought about him regularly and wondered about his motivations. He didn't leave a note or anything, so there was no possible way to understand his motivations at such a young age. It was different for her, at 76 years old. She had started wondering about her utility on the spaceship, and she couldn't help turning the idea of suicide over in her mind. They had a policy in place now, and a procedure to follow, so unlike Kirk, she wouldn't have to do it alone, and there would be no guilt over wasted resources.

The day that Voyager 4 passed Voyager 3 in 2043 was a momentous event for the crew that had departed in 1977. They hadn't seen signs of life outside of the shuttle since they left Earth and certainly nothing resembling the newly designed STS. It was beautiful and sleek. It looked like a roadster compared to the chunky Big-G they were traveling in. Amelia was the first to see the ship, and she didn't say anything initially. She just took it in. In part, it was so far away she wasn't sure what it was. Then, when it was closer, she had a good idea that it was indeed a spaceship, and yet she still kept it to herself. After a few moments of marveling at it, Amelia told the others, and then everyone wanted to crowd around the glass. They all knew it was a ridiculous desire, but collectively the team wished they had a horn, or something to make noise to call attention to themselves, but they didn't have a horn. No spacecraft did. They waved and jumped up and down, and then the ship passed them, and disappeared into the darkness. It felt like a collective dream.

The Voyager 4 team left Earth in 2001. When it passed Voyager 3, it was more puzzling to the crew than anything. To them, the older craft was a space anomaly. Where had it come from? They saw no signs of life and assumed it was an old abandoned craft or space waste, and so they returned their focus to their mission without giving it much more' thought. Realistically, there were tens of thousands of pieces of space waste, abandoned lander modules, spent boosters, errant satellites, and that didn't even include probes, like Pioneer 6, 7, and 8, or the International Cometary Explorer that had stopped responding years ago. Voyager 3 wasn't officially on the books, so nobody on board Voyager 4 was expecting it or looking for it. Additionally, Voyager 3 had been retrofitted from an older craft and then constructed as a prototype, so it didn't look like anything else that had been launched before. While it most closely resembled the Gemini-era spacecraft, most of the crew of Voyager 4 hadn't been born when the Gemini program ended in 1966. It's understandable the Voyager 4 crew missed the passing resemblance.

Voyager 3 was a modified prototype of the "advanced Big G." At the time it was adapted, it was a huge leap forward in terms of the number of crew members it could carry. The "Big G" would have held nine, and the "advanced Big G" had space for twelve. When the decision was made to go ahead with the Voyager 3 mission, the team altered the prototype to make as much living space as possible. The original design called for "cargo space" because the plan was to take materials into orbit or to attach to a space station, but since this spaceship was now headed to the ends of the known solar system, there was no need for cargo. The space was converted into a combination of living space, food, oxygen, and the essentials for life. The plan was to start with four crew members and raise another 4-6 crew members at a time. NASA felt there was plenty of room for this number of passengers. Compared to Voyager 4, which could accommodate sixty-six crew members, food, oxygen, essentials, and living space, Voyager 3 was a dinosaur.

The crew of Voyager 4 didn't recognize the outdated spacecraft in front of them, but the original crew members of Voyager 3 had a pretty good idea what had just passed them. The Voyager 4 didn't look exactly like the early drafts from 1972, but it was close enough that the crew knew what they were looking at. It was a manned spaceship, headed in the same direction as they were, only moving much, much faster, with newer technology, and likely on the same mission. Voyager 3 had lost communication with Earth decades ago.

The new spacecraft was a revelation for the crew that had been born during the mission. Their only experience with human made things was what they saw around them, and yet they immediately recognized the STS as being of Earth. What they didn't understand was why it was passing them and not making any attempt to make communication.

"Why aren't they stopping?" asked Sidney.

"We can't be sure there's anyone on board," said Hugh carefully. "It may be unmanned."

"I'm pretty sure I saw a human on board," said Edgar. "And, besides, it's going awfully fast for something that's unmanned."

"Just because it started out manned, doesn't mean there's still life aboard," suggested Hugh.

"Well, that would explain why there was no effort to contact us from them," said Eva.

That seemed to settle the crew for the most part, but Amelia and Edgar weren't convinced. After the rest of the group dispersed from the window, Amelia and Edgar lingered and approached Hugh and Arnold.

"I'm done," said Edgar.

"Me, too," said Amelia.

"With what?" asked Hugh. He was genuinely surprised.

"With the mission," said Amelia. She was speaking for them both now. Edgar hadn't talked to her about it, but she knew what was on his mind. "Look, I'm seventy-six. I've taught all I can teach, and we're running out of room. Edgar, I can't speak for him exactly, but I'm sure he's feeling a little

77

hopeless given what we've just witnessed."

"Just what did we witness?" asked Hugh.

"Don't bullshit them," said Arnold. "You know, it's a fucking spaceship with newer technology, more room, and faster. Even if we do get to complete our mission, they'll beat us to the punch."

Edgar nodded at Arnold. "What he said," Edgar nodded at Amelia and added, "and what she said. I'll only add that my maleness adds nothing to this mission. So, I'm done."

The two additional suicides shook the remaining crew, and Hugh, Arnold, and Opal had to work hard to convince the others to stem the flow of copycats. This was a hard path to row. They had to convince the remaining crew, all women, that it was still a worthwhile mission.

They also didn't know how long their lives would be. They had theorized that without gravity tugging on bones and organs people might live longer in space, but for a long time, it had all been just a theory. It wasn't until 2066 when Hugh was still alive at the incredible age of 125 and the surviving original crew was also in their one-hundreds, that the theory was confirmed. When Hugh finally died twenty-nine years later, it was proven to be more than just good genes that got him past one hundred. The crew that was born on board would live even longer, giving them more time to contemplate life and its meaning, and whether the mission was worthwhile or not.

7—VOYAGER 4: 2001 (COMPILED FROM NASA DOCUMENTS AND ORAL HISTORIES)

Voyager 4 was formally, officially, named Voyager 77. Those on board weren't privy to the launch of Voyager 3. The basic design of Voyager 77 was the same as any of the other space shuttle orbital vehicles built from 1976-1991, and so it made sense to select a name using the same name-scheme. Most of the other space shuttles—Challenger (1978), Columbia (1979), Discovery (1983), Atlantis (1985), and Endeavour (1991)—were named after sailing ships. These ships had some kind of military purpose before being converted to exploration and discovery, and it was this "second life" for which the space shuttles were named after their sea-bound namesakes.

The original Voyager was going to be named Constitution, but hundreds of thousands of Star Trek fans protested, and President Ford ultimately was convinced to pay homage to the TV show. The only other space shuttle to have a quirky story behind its name was Endeavour. Endeavour, built in 1976, was named after a fictional vessel. The shuttle was designed to replace the Challenger, and since so many children had witnessed the Challenger explosion live on television, many while at school, NASA created a national competition for children to name its replacement shuttle. Endeavour, one of Captain James Cook's ships, was selected as the winner. Since Cook was English, they went with the English spelling of the name, and thus the "u" in Endeavour.

The team in charge of christening Voyager 4 considered several names. One team member wanted to break with tradition and name the shuttle after a tool for navigation—astrolabe, or sunstone—but that was quickly shot down. Both tools were useful for astronomical measurements, but this was a multigenerational space ship that would delve into space in a way no human had before. A tool, regardless of how powerful or novel, wouldn't be a suitable namesake for such an important mission.

"What about Lindberg's plane?"

"The Spirit of St. Louis?"

"Well, we could drop the St. Louis and just go with Spirit."

"But it only traveled across the Atlantic."

"It broke new ground!"

"Next."

"The Canary? Earhart's plane?"

"She disappeared and never completed her flight around the globe!"

Ferdinand Magellan was considered as a patron saint of the mission. He died before the end of his mission, but some of his crew were successful. Some members of the team actually liked that the original captain didn't complete the mission because the space flight would be completed by a later generation, but none of the names of Magellan's ships were particularly inspiring. None of the team members knew what name-scheme Magellan had used to come up with San Antonio, Concepcion, Santiago, Victoria, and Trinidad, but they knew these were all Spanish names—Magellan was funded by Charles V of Spain after all—but even their translated names were not particularly striking. Plus, the only ship that Magellan actually had commanded was the Trinidad, and none of the crew thought "trinity" was as inspiring as Magellan must have thought it was. For a short time, they also considered naming the space shuttle Magellan, but then they learned more about the explorer and realized he was barely more palatable than Christopher Columbus.

Finally, a team member brought in an old newspaper clipping that had been used as a long-forgotten bookmark. The story in the clipping was about the Rutan Model 76 Voyager, piloted by Dick Rutan and Jeana Yeager (no relation to Chuck Yeager, despite their shared love of aviation), that had traveled around the world without stopping or refueling in just nine days.

That team member, whose name has been forgotten by time, declared, "Just like our mission. No stopping or refueling! Except for instead of just around the globe, this is across the universe."

There was some confusion from the other team members as they asked, "Rutan? What the hell is a Rutan?"

And others who complained that "Rutan Model 76 Voyager" was too long and unwieldy.

Eventually, the owner of the bookmark clarified the suggestion. "No, you idiots; you're thinking too concretely. The name we need has been staring us in the face the whole time: Voyager. That's what all the other deep-space crafts are called. We'll call this one Voyager 77, a kind of homage to the launch year of the first Voyagers. Plus, it will be like Rutan Model 76 + 1. Get it? 77 is one more than 76? And this is a bigger mission?"

While that last comment caused a bit of a stir—because, really, only plus 1? Voyager 77 would be traveling much further than Voyager 76 without refueling or stopping—ultimately it was decided. The new space shuttle would be called Voyager 77, though it would actually be the fourth Voyager. One find dissenting voice argued that it would be confusing for a spacecraft to be named Voyager 77 and its maiden voyage would take place in 2001, but the die had already been cast—Voyager 77 it was.

While plenty of thought went into naming the craft, and the team working on launching Voyager 77 did their best to anticipate the needs of the crew (current and future) as best as they could. No one could have predicted how miserable it would be to raise babies, much less toddlers or teenagers, in space. Even under the best circumstances, with the most patient and experienced adults, it would have been extremely difficult. As with the crew of Voyager 3, none of the members of Voyager 77 had any parental experience. Worse, they had no desire to ever become parents.

Unfortunately, the cross-section of people interested in multigenerational space travel and interested in having children and parenting is quite small. While NASA had sought single people to pilot their craft into the unknown, people without attachments and "nothing to lose," they had unwittingly found the worst-suited persons to deal with the frustrations of parenting. None of the chosen crew were located within the overlap in that Venn diagram.

NASA worked hard to prepare the crew for anything they might face in space, but they found it impossible to acquire a baby to use in simulations. Had this been a public space flight, it might have been reasonable for the organization to find a willing set of parents to have their child raised—at least in part—by astronauts. But it wasn't. The skeletal team organizing Voyager 77 did what they could with baby dolls and books and videos, and then crossed their fingers and hoped that some kind of paternal and maternal instincts would kick in.

The two oldest members of the Voyager 77 crew, Zach Sheridan (35) and Zina Watson (36) were also the least tolerant of children. Both believed their age and seniority, not to mention their status as co-captains, granted them immunity to any child-related duties. They knew that raising the "next generation" was part of the overall mission; they just didn't feel as though children were part of *their* job. Their role was to navigate and maintain the ship and to take charge of assigned observation duties and experiments. Not surprisingly, they always seemed to have essential duties to attend to whenever children cried or needed to be changed.

It didn't help that Zina and Zach were both intense introverts who had never formed a circle of friends like most people do in high school. Zina was content with her two or three close friends and her collection of early-80s goth records. Between Joy Division, The Cure, Bauhaus, her friends, and her books, Zina was rarely ever lonely. Zach was similarly surrounded by a small circle of friends, but instead of listening to "the mopers and dopers" (as he called the goths), he was into Judas Priest, Motorhead, Iron Maiden, and a new band Metallica, which he discovered and fell in love with during the summer of his senior year.

As their friends changed and evolved with the times, neither Zina nor Zach ever shook the music that formed their personalities in high school. People in graduate school gave Zach shit for his love of thrash and speed metal, and Zina was similarly mocked for her wardrobe of mostly black. Their preferred genres of music might have put Zina and Zach at odds with one another, but their shared dislike of children and attachment to music from their high school days brought them together. As co-captains, they were a united front: Child-related duties were delegated to the lower ranks.

Isiah Heller (33) was the only member of the crew who had a younger brother and actually remembered changing diapers to help his parents. Since Freddy was eleven years younger than Isiah, it often fell to him to babysit, change diapers, and feed his little brother. Isiah might have put up a fight when his parents asked for his help, but in truth he loved the little guy and was happy to help. Plus, it quickly became one of Isiah's chores, which meant he got paid for it. Money and time with his little brother? Hard to top that. Who knew that those experiences would come in handy when he agreed to push off into space on a mission of unknown duration?

As a kid, Isiah didn't think diapers were so bad. He could always wash his hands if something got on him. The bigger problem was being protected from Freddy's sudden unexpected release of bodily fluids. On Earth, it was messy, but it was easily cleaned. In space, Isiah learned quickly, pee not only went everywhere, it also simply floated away. Cleaning up wasn't as simple as wiping down a wall or a surface, and it wasn't like he could just grab the floating urine. Instead, he had to envelope it or capture it with something and let it soak in. Then he had to clean the object that had soaked up the urine. It was quite the ordeal.

It didn't take long for Isiah to realize just how spoiled he had been with disposable diapers on Earth. Disposable diapers would have been great to have on board, but they didn't have the storage for them. Even if they could afford to set aside enough room for disposable diapers for the entire duration of the next generation's diapering needs, there was no way there would be enough room for diapers for any generation thereafter. Additionally, in this tightly controlled, closed system, there was no room for waste. Everything had to be repurposed. Disposable diapers flew in the face of that mandate. Needless to say, Isiah couldn't wait for the next generation—Mabel and Bonnie, both born in 2002—to be potty trained.

It shouldn't have been a surprise then when just as diapering proved more difficult than on Earth, potty training was even more so. The crew knew the bladder behaved differently in zero gravity, but until they had actually experienced it, they didn't fully appreciate the differences. Without gravity there is no pressure to tell you that your bladder is full.

An adult bladder can hold up to sixteen ounces of urine comfortably and, on Earth, pressure tells you that you should go when it hits that level. You can hold it longer, but by the time you get to twenty ounces, it's time to go. Theoretically, a bladder can hold nearly two liters—67.6 ounces—but it creates serious discomfort. John Glenn, the holder of many "firsts" for NASA, was also the first to realize the bladder in space wouldn't be creating pressure to indicate that it was time to go. Glenn figured he had a full bladder, but even he was surprised when he peed twenty-seven ounces during his first orbital flight. After that incident, NASA knew to alert astronauts to make an effort to urinate every three to four hours since their bodies wouldn't alert them naturally.

All this is to say, the early years of raising a child on board a spaceship were extremely difficult; this meant the crew of Voyager 77 limited the number of children to the lowest possible number. Even if the crew had loved children, they would have limited the number of offspring due to space constraints. Mabel and Bonnie were both born in 2002, and neither of them reproduced until they were in their thirties. By that time, Isiah was out of practice with diapering and potty training, and he and the rest of the crew (minus Zina and Zach who still stubbornly refused to have anything to do with children) had to stumble through it all over again. When Mabel gave birth to Salvador, there was a shared disappointment that they would have to go through it all again for chance at a female. Bonnie aligned with Zach and Zina and wanted nothing to do with children; she refused to even be inseminated. This left the burden to Mabel to try again for a female offspring. She waited two years, and in 2037 she gave birth to Joanna, and the fate of the mission was back on track.

An unexpected benefit of zero gravity was that the whole spaceship was essentially baby proof. Everything had a lid. Everything had a secured location, so it wouldn't drift away. The crew had thought to bring some children's toys, but anyone born aboard was treated more like mini-adults than children. "Toys" were usually tools or essential items that had been repurposed into objects of entertainment for the babies. On the plus side, no one would ever complain about stepping on LEGOs (and without gravity, they wouldn't have been sprinkled on the floor had they been on the ship anyway).

While there was no crawling or first steps, there was plenty of cruising. Thanks to the lack of gravity, children were incredibly mobile. Baby Joanna, especially, was adept at navigating the spacecraft from an early age. Once she mastered her pincher grip at seven months, it was hard to know where that child would wind up. Mabel and Bonnie were much more accustomed to the mode of transportation than any of the adults on board, since they had been born on the craft, but even they had a hard time keeping up with the energetic child. Thankfully, Johanna would run out of juice before too long or become bored with the limited places she could go.

Once the children were five years old, they passed the time doing the things most of the adults did. If the launch had taken place in November 2001, the ship could have been outfitted with an XBOX, but because it launched in May, the crew had to make do with the PlayStation 2, which was being phased out at the time with only a handful of new games available the PS2. Thankfully, there were plenty of PS1 games to choose from, which worked on the updated system.

True to their immutable natures, Zina and Zach cared not a whit for the technology of video games. They each had been exposed to video games, but they found the "new" controllers to have too many buttons and to be too clumsy to navigate successfully. Occasionally, boredom or the goading of another crew member would incite Zach or Zina to play, but the experience—being destroyed in *Tekken* or any number of sports games, or not being able to keep the beat in *PaRappa the Rapper*—only reinforced their disdain for the technology.

"Besides," said Zach, one day after having his ass handed to him in *Quake II* by Nelda, "why waste your time on this, when there's so much outside to observe?"

Nelda Crist was the second youngest of the original crew, and was, hands down, the best video game player on Voyager 4. She glanced out the window and said, "all that? You mean the same crap we see every hour, every minute, every second of every day? Yeah, I'll pass. At least the game is different each time we play."

This was a point of contention between Zach and Nelda. Zach couldn't understand why an astronaut would sign up for a historic mission and then turn his or her gaze away from the stars ever. Nelda couldn't wrap her brain around how Zach was content to stare at the same stars and planets endlessly.

"I think," Nelda said, not for the first time, "you simply lack the hand-eye coordination to master the controller and," she paused to make sure he was listening and waited to catch his eye, "you can't keep a beat."

Jolanda Short, the youngest of the crew, was not typically one to defend Zach, but on this occasion, she found herself on his side. "Look," she said, "keeping a beat shouldn't be a requirement of any video game. That's just silly."

"Thank you," Zach said.

"Oh come on," Nelda tapped her foot and recited "Chop Chop Master Onion's Rap" to her beat, "Kick! Punch! It's all in the mind / if you wanna test me, I'm sure you'll find / the things I teach ya is sure to beat ya / nevertheless you'll get a lesson from teacher now."

"See, you're making the argument for me now. Why would you have that ridiculous rhyme memorized?" Zach asked. "How does that serve the mission?"

"It serves to keep me entertained," said Nelda.

Jolanda couldn't argue with that. "Look, you two; we all have different ways of staying sane on this trip. Can we just agree to each their own?"

In addition to the PS2, the crew also had laptops. Jolanda and Zina each had an Apple PowerBook G4, and Zach, Isiah, and Nelda had Compaq Presarios. The CPU on the PlayStation 2 only ran at 294 MHz, and each laptop either doubled (or nearly doubled) that speed. The laptops had far more RAM, but the graphics on the PS2 were far superior. For the gamers, there was no competition when it came to the interface. On Earth, PC versions of most PS2 games were being produced, but anyone who had played a game on each platform preferred the PS2 version without question.

The laptops were only occasionally used for games (mostly Solitaire, Free Cell, and Minesweeper), but more often they were used for taking notes, making spreadsheets, and watching DVDs. When the primary television wasn't being used for videogames, the crew would gather around and collectively watch a movie. More often, the television was tied up with gaming, which meant the crew regularly watched DVDs on their laptops privately. The invention of the DVD allowed the crew to bring a library of films to choose from. Without that leap of technology, the film library would have been dramatically reduced in number because VHS tapes took up so much space.

The original crew had their differences about the value of videogames, but they all agreed that films were a lifesaver. Everyone enjoyed watching a movie. They each had their preferences—Zina preferred documentaries, Zach was a sucker for a good drama, Isiah loved apocalyptic movies of all kinds, Jolanda loved slap-stick comedy, and Nelda's favorite was a good bio-pic—but if someone was watching any film on the television, they would all settle in to enjoy it. Even if someone didn't "like" a film, they usually found something redeemable to say about it. Sometimes it inspired conversations about films they didn't have in the ship's library.

"I really don't understand why they never released *The Wild Life* on DVD," said Zach. "That was a great film."

"Great is really overselling it," said Jolanda.

Zach looked surprised. "You've seen it?"

"I know I haven't," said Isiah. He could see where this discussion was headed and bowed out of it before it really got going. Instead, he found a nook in another room and opened a book. He didn't have the same photographic memory in regard to film and actors as the rest of the crew to actively participate in these conversations.

"Just because I'm the youngest, doesn't mean I don't have a taste for cinema," Jolanda pressed.

"Huh," said Zach. "But, you were like, what? Eight when it came out?"

"Even though it wasn't released on DVD, it was released on VHS," Jolanda said. "Plus, it might have helped that I had a film appreciation class, and its focus was cinema of 1984."

"No shit?" asked Nelda. She was suddenly interested in the discussion.

"I thought it would be some easy credits and a chance to see movies, like the Godfather again. I didn't know I'd be immersed in the 80s."

"What other movies did you 'appreciate'?" asked Zach.

"Ghostbusters, Romancing the Stone, The Search for Spock, Amadeus, Repo Man, The Killing Fields, Buckaroo Banzai Across the 8th Dimension, and, *The Natural,"* Jolanda said.

"That's quite the list," said Zach. "No *Beverly Hills Cop?* Or *Sixteen Candles?* Or *Splash?"*

"What about the *Last Starfighter?"* asked Zina

The three suddenly turned and looked at their fourth crew member. The silence formed a collective "huh?" in the cabin.

"What?" asked Zina. "That was my favorite film from 1984. And as astronauts, I guess I thought you would appreciate it, too."

"Fair enough," said Jolanda. "I never gave the 'cinema of 1984' much thought until that class, but you're right; there's a lot to choose from that year."

"Against All Odds, Elm Street, The Terminator, Revenge of the Nerds," Zach continued listing films.

"Was *Gremlins* 1984?" asked Nelda.

"Yes, so was *Temple of Doom,"* added Jolanda.

"And *Red Dawn,"* said Zina. *"The Woman in Red, Karate Kid, Top Secret."*

"That was a terrible movie," said Zach.

"No, I think it was just misunderstood. There are some great comedic moments in it," countered Jolanda.

"Wait, which one are we talking about? Are we still talking about *The Wild Life?"* asked Nelda.

Jolanda laughed. "No, *Top Secret."*

"Is that the one with Dan Aykroyd and Chevy Chase?" asked Zina.

"You're thinking of *Spies Like Us,"* said Zach. *"Top Secret* was by the *Airplane* guys, and it had Val Kilmer in it."

"Oh," said Zina. "I think *Footloose* was 1984. And maybe *The Neverending Story?"*

"Dune and *Spinal Tap,* too," said Jolanda.

"Did anyone say *A Passage to India* yet?" asked Nelda.

"Holy shit, you could make like six sections of Cinema of 1984 and offer respectable film lists for each," said Zach.

"So, what was so special about *The Wild Life?*" asked Nelda. "I've never seen it."

"For starters, it was Cameron Crowe's follow-up to *Fast Times*," said Zach. "I love everything Crowe did."

"I've seen that movie, and I know that name, but I can't place it," said Zina.

"*Singles? Say Anything?*" Jolanda said.

"More like *Jerry Maguire* and just before we left Earth, *Almost Famous*," said Nelda.

"Oh, he did *Jerry Maguire?*" asked Zina. "I loved that movie."

"The problem with *The Wild Life*," said Jolanda, bringing the conversation back to its focus, "is that it's basically a rehash of everything Fast Times did much better, and with better actors, and a better soundtrack."

"Hey! Eddie Van Halen did the score for *Wild Life!*" said Zach.

"Oh, right, and 'Donut City' is such a great song." Jolanda laughed. "He should stick with Mr. Roth to make music. Or even Mr. Hagar."

"I'll grant you that," said Zach. "But *Wild Life* has Chris Penn (Sean's brother), Rick Moranis, Lea Thompson, and Eric Stoltz. That's a solid cast."

"Geez, and you get on Nelda for wasting her time with video games," said Zina. "How much worthless knowledge about movies do you have in that brain of yours?"

Zach almost responded about how all information was vital for the mission, no matter how small or seemingly irrelevant it was. Future generations needed to know where they came from and what values, including entertainment, their forefathers and foremothers held, and what made them the kind of people they were. He could have gone on and on about other films, like *Dudes* (1987) and how it also hadn't been released on DVD or the *Let It Be* documentary which was being held up by George Harrison and Yoko Ono. But he kept his thoughts to himself and left the shared space. Not releasing Penelope Spheeris's *Dudes*, which formed a sort of conclusion to her trilogy of music films beginning with *The Decline of Western Civilization* (1981) and followed by *Suburbia* (1984), was a real shame, because it traced the evolution of LA's music scene transitioning from punk to heavy metal. Zach loved metal. But, if there were a musical time capsule Zach had wished they could bring for future generations, it would have been *Let It Be*. It documented The Beatles recording what would be their final release. There was footage of rehearsals, the band members laughing and bickering, and, in short, some of Earth's best musicians creating an iconic album. Sadly, the VHS had been out of print for a long time, and no DVD release was in time to make the trip.

When it came to the crew members born in space, movies were considered deeply informational. These films were a glimpse at a planet they would never see first-hand. Mabel and Bonnie didn't understand why the original crew members panned some films and made fun of the girls for putting up with "bad acting." For them, there was no bad acting; it was simply a different perspective of human behavior. Had they not been told better, they would have assumed the "acting" in *Howard the Duck* (1986) or *Superman IV* (1987) or *The Garbage Pail Kids* (1987) or *Mac and Me* (1988) or *Highlander 2* (1991) or *Batman & Robin* (1997) was simply how some people were normally.

The default expectation when watching a film was that it was a true story, until one of the older crew members reminded the younger crew members that many films were fiction. Regardless of how many times they were reminded of this, Mabel and Bonnie thought of characters as real, historical people. Since they watched the films so many times throughout their lives, these fictional memories eventually became ingrained into their minds as "real" experiences replacing the lack of real experiences they had of their own.

One day Zina walked in on Mabel telling baby Salvador a story and was horrified to hear Mabel's account of President Maverick and how he was elected because he fought off the Communists. Zina resisted the urge to immediately correct her and instead waited to hear the rest of the story.

"It was too bad that his best friend, Goose," Mabel said, "died before he could see Maverick become president."

Whatever she had to say about the accuracy of such a story, it did seem to put baby Salvador to sleep. Zina waited for Mabel to finish zipping Salvador into his sleep sack and then caught her arm as Mabel propelled herself out of the sleeping quarters. She'd had time to think about what she would say to Mabel, but still hadn't come up with anything she was particularly proud of.

"Fan fiction of *Top Gun*?" she asked.

Her voice, though quiet, startled Mabel and she drifted into a wall. "What's fan fiction?" she finally asked.

Ultimately, Mabel laughed off the story. "You know babies; you can tell them anything in the right voice and they'll smile. Or fall asleep to it."

"But, you know Maverick and Goose aren't real people. Right?" Zina pressed.

"Of course."

The problem was, the stories that the original crew members told them weren't as compelling or entertaining or memorable as the fictional ones they enjoyed on DVD. It didn't matter that one set of "stories" (or histories) were true and another were not; it was a matter of which they found more quotable, or worth repeating, or wanting to engage more with. It wasn't entirely the fault of the original crew. None of them were gifted actors with the opportunity of multiple takes or a director coaching from the sidelines or a team of writers to give them the best possible lines. These were simply people who had lived on Earth, who had obtained advanced degrees and studied hard, and who were doing their best to pass on a complex set of intertwining narrative histories. The starting point was always Eurocentric, because each crew member was from the United States. They did their best to educate the younger generations about the rest of the world, but the most nuanced discussions were about the history of the United States, and any conflict was told through an American lens.

Understandably, for Mabel, Bonnie, Salvador, Joanna, and finally Omar, the sixteenth president of the United States was just as abstract as Lt. Pete "Maverick" Mitchell or LTJG Nick "Goose" Bradshaw.

By the time Omar was born in 2070, the blurring of fact and fiction was complete. Joanna, Mabel's final child, had been raised on her love of *Top Gun* and other quasi-romantic films. She also recounted the versions of American history that she'd been told, but she lacked the conviction and experience on Earth to sell these "stories" to her offspring. As a result, Omar's history of Earth was fully confused. Zach and Zina, or Isiah, Jolanda, Nelda, could have offered a course correction for the little guy, but they had grown old and felt they had done a sufficient enough job of passing down the oral histories over the previous decades. By then, the tedium of the mission had worn them down, and the original crew kept mostly to themselves.

Joanna's announcement that she would not be having another child shook the crew. Joanna had been spending time with Bonnie and found the second female born on board to be a wonderful mentor. Mabel (Joanna's birth mother), had discouraged Joanna from spending much time with Bonnie because the crew believed that Bonnie hated children. This was only partly true. The truth was that Bonnie didn't fully understand what a child was, and when she was told she was expected to produce one, she was afraid and resistant. Once Mabel gave birth to Salvador, Bonnie found she was fascinated by the miniature person and loved watching him develop. The birthing process, however, still terrified her. So, she stood by her original claim that she didn't want to have children, and Mabel was asked to be fertilized to produce another child— hopefully a female. It went as hoped, and little Joanna was born.

Bonnie remained on the sidelines as Joanna grew and developed, but when the rest of the crew receded into their isolation, it was Bonnie who reached out to a twenty-something Joanna. The two spoke regularly. Finally, one day Joanna asked Bonnie why she had refused to be fertilized.

"It's simply really," Bonnie said. "It was such a foreign thing to me. I just didn't understand, and they didn't exactly broach the topic with much care or tenderness. It was all about how important the mission was, and how I was expected, because I was female, to keep the mission alive. I didn't ask to be on the mission. Zach, Isiah, Zina and them, they made a choice to leave Earth. None of us made the choice to be astronauts, much less mothers. That felt like a choice I could make, and so I did."

The logic resonated with Joanna.

While the first children—Mabel and Bonnie—were born only a year after Voyager 4 took flight, Salvador was born when Mabel was thirty-three. Mabel waited another two years before giving birth to Joanna. There was a general consensus that since humans would (probably) live longer in space, it was also reasonable to assume women could give birth later without the complications geriatric pregnancies faced on Earth. Thus, no pressure was exerted on Joanna to be fertilized until she passed thirty-five. Now suddenly there was concern.

"What do you mean you don't want to have a baby?" asked Zach.

"This isn't an option," said Zina.

"Hold on there now," said Bonnie. "Of course, it's a choice."

"I'm just not ready yet," said Joanna. "I'm not saying no forever, but I'm not ready. Yet."

Eventually their insistence wore Joanna down, and she agreed to be fertilized. Omar was born shortly after Joanna turned thirty-four. Since the baby was a boy, Zach and Zina immediately began to pressure Joanna to try again. While they both believed in the extended fertility that space (probably) offered, neither was willing to risk experimenting until they had multiple viable females. Mabel and Bonnie were now both in their early seventies, and everyone believed that was pushing the limits of whatever extended-fertility the lack of gravity might provide. To their surprise, Joanna held firm.

"No," she said. "Not again. I won't doom anyone to this life without a choice."

"Instead you're going to doom all of us?" asked Zach.

"That's not fair to put it all on her," said Isiah. He loved little Omar. Somehow the birth of this little boy brought out the paternal instincts he once exhibited with Mabel and Bonnie. Even though Omar had darker skin than Isiah's brother Freddy, Isiah couldn't help but look at the little guy and think of his brother. What was Freddy up to now? Isiah was one hundred and nine, which meant Freddy would be ninety eight. It suddenly hit Isiah that his brother might not still be alive, and that made his connection with Omar even stronger.

"Look. I get that it's your choice and all," said Zina. "But a lot is riding on this. We need another female, or two, but at least one, to keep this mission going. Otherwise, this will all be for nothing."

"I'm sorry," said Joanna. She felt particularly guilty for Mabel, the woman who had birthed her because Mabel also hadn't asked to be an astronaut, or a mother, and yet she had become both. "I just can't do it. This is a miserable existence."

"She's not wrong," said Nelda. "At least on Earth you had options. What kind of options do you have here?"

"Lots of movies and videogames," said Jolanda.

"And being a vessel for children," said Bonnie.

"You did this, didn't you?" asked Zach, glaring at Bonnie.

Bonnie held up her hands. "I can't help it if she doesn't value your mission the way you do."

Omar became the last baby born on Voyager 4 in 2070. Zach and Zina spoke privately about the possibility of forced fertilization. Had they been younger or had a better sense of how much longer the lack of gravity would extend their lives, they might have more seriously pursued it. But, even if they had managed to forcefully fertilize Joanna, the younger crew could refuse to pilot the ship, or veer off course, or mutiny.

Instead, the crew shifted their focus away from coercing

Joanna to bear an offspring and instead considered what their options going forward could be. Do they turn around? Could they produce a child another way? They had frozen eggs and sperm; it was possible they could use the womb of an older female crew member to simply house the fetus. Maybe Mabel would be willing to experiment? Or maybe they would simply soldier on and see how long they could all live and how far they'd get.

(PS: henceforth, let's forgo the formalities of referring to Voyager 77 by its proper name, and stick with its chronological name of Voyager 4—even though, yes, I am aware Voyager 2 launched before Voyager 1, so it's not truly chronological. Don't worry, this will all become only slightly more confusing when a fifth Voyager is launched a few chapters later.)

8—RESEARCH IN SPACE (COMPLIED FROM THE CASSETTE AND VIDEO JOURNALS OF CREW MEMBERS)

Voyager 3 and Voyager 4 were both "off the book" missions, and the passengers of both ships were led to believe that communication with Earth was impossible. What most did not know was that each ship did in fact have a radio, but it was only to be used when the mission was completed. An "or if" in the directive for use might have been implied, but it was never stated. In order to keep panicked, bored, or disenchanted passengers from signaling, the radio was kept secret. Only the crew captain and co-captain knew about its existence, and it was up to them to determine the members of the next generations to tell.

On Voyager 3, Hugh and Arnold passed the information onto Kirk. When Kirk killed himself, Hugh and Arnold held onto the secret until they found another mission-loyal soul in the third generation – Amber. On Voyager 77, Zach and Zina skipped the first generation born in space entirely; they just didn't like Mabel or Bonnie; instead, they chose Salvador. They realized putting all their eggs in one basket was risky, but they simply didn't feel as though anyone else valued the mission enough to reward them with such an important piece of it.

When Joanna refused to reproduce again after Omar was born, two things were confirmed. First, Zach and Zina had made a good decision in withholding this information from Joanna, and second, it didn't matter because the mission was now doomed.

One perk of being on an unofficial mission, if there were really any worth mentioning, was neither crew was burdened with the expectation to complete experiments while on board. Any other mission would require its crew to perform various functions in space and report back to NASA. Since there was no means of communication with NASA, there was no need to perform experiments. The people putting the launches together didn't feel the need to overcomplicate things by sending the crew with unnecessary equipment to perform tasks they'd never learn the results of anyway. What the planners hadn't counted on was that boredom and tedium of the everyday would drive the crew to perform experiments of their own regardless of expectation or protocol.

As the crews of both ships gazed out the windows looking for any moving thing and watched babies grow and develop over time, they unintentionally all became competent Astrobiologists. Astrobiology would become a "thing" on Earth in 1995. Prior to that, it had been called Exobiology, or Xenobiology. It wasn't until March of 1995 that Wesley Huntress suggested a focused study of "life in the universe" and that the study would be called Astrobiology.

In the meantime, the crews of the Voyager ships checked and recorded their pulses, temperatures, and blood pressures on a daily basis. In the early days of the flight, Hugh, Arnold, Amelia, and Opal compared notes. In general, everyone presented the same findings. Blood pressure and pulse were down and body temperature was up. They attributed lower blood pressure and pulses to eating a better diet and decreased stress levels.

"I mean, other than knowing we're going to die in space," Arnold once joked.

"It takes some of the mystery out of it," said Amelia. "At least you know where."

But the body temperature surprised them. It was the equivalent of perpetually running a low-grade fever. Every day, it was 38 degrees Celsius or 100.4 Fahrenheit (plus or minus a fraction of a degree).

"What's the deal?" asked Hugh.

"Increased radiation levels?" suggested Amelia.

"Could be," said Arnold. "Or, maybe our body isn't as good at releasing heat in space for some reason?"

"I don't know what it is, but I hate always feeling generally shitty. Not terrible, but you know," said Hugh.

And they did. Everyone felt a little off. There wasn't much they could do about it, and they needed to preserve the medication they had for more serious matters. Over time they got used to functioning a little hotter than usual with lower blood pressure and decreased heart rate.

By the time Voyager 4 went up, the new crew had a better understanding of how the body reacts to space conditions. For example, they knew that the heart doesn't have to work as hard to circulate blood in space. Voyager 4 also knew the heart, just like all muscles in the human body, would atrophy from not having gravity pull against it. They had seen plenty astronauts return from extended stays in space with the fat heads and bloated chests from excess blood not circulating, as well as the chicken legs that had atrophied as a result of blood not being pumped to the extremities.

The more interesting data for both crews emerged when the next generations were born in space. This was something new to compare their results against. Interestingly, none of the space-born crew members seemed to suffer from the same symptoms associated with low-grade fevers. Blood pressure and heartrate were consistent with the numbers of the Earth-born crew members, too. All in all, the new crew members seemed healthy and happy. Just like the other crew members, their numbers were fairly consistent and regular with each other.

Unfortunately, self-evaluation of basic functions was the limit of either crews' ability to evaluate their overall health. Space constraints at the time of launches meant no attempt was made to equip the crews with radiology (or PET or CAT or CT scan) equipment or anything that might give a clearer picture of what was going on inside the body. The Voyager 77 crew knew that bone density loss was a common side effect of extended stays in space, but without equipment to properly examine the actual loss, they were unsure of what years in space would do to their bodies versus the few months of the astronauts they had studied before leaving Earth. Had they had that kind of equipment, they would have identified significant decreases in bone density and volume of blood in the circulatory system.

Instead, the majority of the experiments (or, perhaps observations is a better word for it) occurred outside of the ships. At first, it was the novelty of seeing Earth disappear that drew the astronauts' eyes. Then it became a game of trying to spot Earth, but soon the planet was indistinguishable or simply lost in the void. Attention was then redirected to identifying which planet they were approaching or passing, and then observations were made of the planet and radiation levels were recorded. In between planets, stargazing occurred. Notes were made, and star charts were drawn.

One day, Amelia was convinced she saw something approaching the ship. At first, she didn't say anything, because she didn't want to unnecessarily alarm anyone, but eventually she called Opal over to take a look.

"See that?" she asked.

"What is that? It looks like a group of something. A formation?" asked Opal.

"That's what I thought," said Amelia.

"Have you shown anyone else?" asked Opal.

"Not yet. I just wanted to make sure I wasn't crazy before I made a big deal out of it." As she twisted her head to turn and call Hugh and Arnold, she saw the formation from a different angle. "Ugh," she grunted. "Never mind."

Opal was still gazing out the window mesmerized by what she saw. "What?"

"Come back here and look," Amelia said.

Opal shifted and joined Amelia. From that vantage point, it was obvious what they had been looking at was a reflection of bolts in the window.

There were other times when the crew saw lights or objects they couldn't explain. Sometimes they heard sounds from outside the ship, which wasn't logical since space is a vacuum. On Voyager 77, Nelda was convinced she had seen eel-like tubes swimming outside one of the windows. None of the other crew members saw them and were convinced she saw some kind of space junk.

"Way out here? Where would the space junk come from?" argued Nelda.

"There are any number of old probes out here," said Jolanda. "Not to mention debris from meteors or comets. Who knows."

"But these were wiggling and moving," Nelda insisted.

The rest of the crew were content to proffer various theories explaining away what Nelda saw—she was overly tired, the debris was moving because space lacked friction to stop it from moving, etc.—but Nelda remained adamant about what she saw that day despite never seeing it again.

Because they were big fans of Eugene Parker's work, Arnold Paul on Voyager 3 and Zina Watson on Voyager 77 made sure to observe and measure solar wind. Passing through the termination shock, then the heliosheath, and then entering the heliopause were remarkable moments for them.

At this point, one might casually assume that the crews' interest in space grew as they passed through the heliopause into the unknown, but instead the crew became increasingly apathetic about their galactic environment and more concerned with their confined space inside the ship. In fact, the crew members born in space never really saw space as anything special; it was simply their reality. The Earth-born crew members struggled to care about space as they aged, and their mortality became more certain. Who could blame them? They had stared out that window at nothing all day every day for years on end. They had been looking at nothing for a long time.

9—SPACE, 2066 (COMPILED FROM THE TESTIMONY OF SURVIVING CREW MEMBERS)

In 2066, Hugh Sullivan turned one hundred and twenty-five years old. He was still the de facto commander on board, but there was little to command or direct, and he became less involved with the day-to-day interactions with the crew. Still, the story that he told years ago, decades ago, was still being retold. Maggie, who was now thirty-two had heard it from her birth-mother, Eva, who had heard it from her birth-mother Rebecca, who had heard it from Hugh first-hand back in 1989 when she was ten.

Maggie was telling the story to the ten-year old twins Kelvin and Kacey. It was the first case, and would be the only case, of twins in space, and no one could explain how it happened. Opal was particularly perplexed because she had studied artificial insemination and couldn't understand how such a controlled environment could produce something as unpredictable, though not necessarily undesirable. As far as Maggie was concerned, twins were the norm. She had never seen anyone else give birth before, so she had nothing to compare it to. And the older crew members hadn't anticipated it as something they'd need to prepare her for.

Maggie adored both of these children. She enjoyed reading to them, but her favorite thing to do was to follow them around. She'd never had a pet or any kind of interactive toy, and the light-hearted engagement with Kelvin and Kacey was completely novel to her. Sometimes the three of them cuddled in the different chambers or played hide and seek, and other times they floated as she told them stories. Some of those stories were made up, and others were ones she had heard before, such as Hugh's story.

"Now Hugh; he always wanted to be an astronaut."

"What's an astronaut?" asked Kelvin.

"We are all astronauts," said Kacey. "Don't you remember?"

"Oh, right," said Kelvin.

"He used to read these very short books with lots of pictures, because he wasn't very good at reading."

"No! You made that part up!" said Kacey. "Hugh likes to read!"

"Back then he only read those picture books. He called them comical books, because the pictures were very silly. But those comical books told about adventures into space."

"That's what we're doing!" said Kelvin.

"Which is why we're astronauts," said Kacey.

"One of the most famous people in these comical space books was Lucy. She always tricked another astronaut named Charlie Brown and made him look stupid. Because he wasn't very smart."

"That's not nice," said Kacey.

"Which part? Saying that he wasn't very smart, or tricking him?"

"Both," said Kelvin.

"Well, Lucy might not have been nice, but she was very famous and one of the superheroes in the comical space books. Back then, it was only through these books that people learned about what space was like."

"Didn't they have space ships?" asked Kacey.

"They were still working on building them. But they did

have telescopes," Rebecca knew they were going to ask, so she immediately added, "which are tubes that allowed them to see far away. And, they used to have different kinds of jobs on Earth. Astronaut was just one job. People could be all kinds of things."

"Like what?" asked Kacey.

"Oh, they used to have people who held footballs—a thing used in a game—and others who made things, and people who spent time thinking about things. All kinds of things."

"We don't have any of those jobs, right?" asked Kelvin. "We're just astronauts."

"Right, but you can do some of those things still. Like, you can definitely spend time thinking. Or you can look out at the stars and planets. And you can write and make things."

"Are we ever going to actually see Earth?" asked Kacey.

"I don't think so. But we'll see lots of other planets and stars on our mission, and one day we'll land a new planet. That's the plan at least."

Opal's stories remained more intact over the years. It was from Opal's account of Earth that Maggie drew heavily to inform her birth-children what the original crew's home planet was like. It was, for the most part, a story of empowerment. Humans had overcome diseases and physical limitations and were the strongest animal on the planet.

"We were so strong, smart, and powerful that we were able to leave our planet. No other animal could do that."

"But, why did we want to leave?" asked Kacey.

That was a harder question to answer because all the stories she had heard about Earth were filled with fond memories. Even Opal, who had suffered discrimination and racial hatred and had been told stories of even worse treatment suffered by her family, still somehow regarded Earth with a strange kind of nostalgia that discolored her memories.

"I think it was because we wanted to see what was out there. To know. To explore. Does that make sense?"

"I guess," said Kelvin. "Seems like a long way to go

105

though."

"I agree. But isn't this kind of neat? Just us here, in this little thing flying through space? I mean, what more could you want?"

The kids didn't know what else they could want because they hadn't anything to compare it to. There were no neighborhood kids who had the best, newest, most expensive toys to envy. There were no commercials to advertise food or toys to desire or places to visit. Kelvin and Kacey, and Maggie for that matter, simply didn't know what else there was to want.

"Can you tell us about the sharks again?" asked Kacey.

Somehow, of all the animals any of the crew had mentioned, sharks were the ones that held tightest to Kacey's imagination.

"Well, they were big. Huge. As big as our ship at least, some were even bigger. And they had massive teeth that could tear you in two." Rebecca knew the kids liked being a little scared but was careful not to overdo it. "The sharks lived in the oceans. These were huge pools of water that were everywhere on the planet. As long as you didn't swim, you didn't encounter any sharks. And even if you did swim, you didn't always find sharks."

"What color were they?" asked Kelvin.

"Gray. Mostly gray."

"But some had white, right?" pressed Kacey.

"Right," Rebecca said, even though she had never seen one and was really only regurgitating what she had been told. "Some did have white. Some were even called the Great Whites. They were the fiercest and meanest."

"No, the whale shark was bigger!" exclaimed Kelvin.

"But the whale shark didn't have big teeth; he ate tiny plants or something," said Kacey.

"Right. There was one great white shark that I read about, and his name was Jaws. He ate so many people, because they all came and swam in his ocean. You'd think with all the teeth, and the fin poking up out of the water, people would learn to stay out of his ocean, but they couldn't stop themselves."

"Why not?" asked Kelvin.

"Because I guess water was fun to be in."

"Fun enough to risk dying?" asked Kacey.

"Yep. They used to take boats out in the ocean, too, and Jaws would get angry and smash their boats."

"Wow," each twin said.

"But, eventually, a guy name Quint killed Jaws and saved this guy Brody, who then told the whole story to everyone."

"It doesn't seem fair," said Kelvin "that they killed Jaws just because they wanted to be in the water. That was his home. They should have let him be safe in his home."

"Humans don't always make the best decisions, and they aren't always nice."

"We're nice, right?" asked Kelvin.

"Are there any space sharks?" interrupted Kacey.

"I don't think so. I think sharks just live on Earth. Why do you ask that?"

"I heard Arnold say something about how the oceans are 'just as vast as space, and we know about as much about them as we do space,' and I just thought maybe the oceans were like where we are. What if there's something that lives in space, and it's his home, and we're in his home, like people were in Jaws' home."

"Then we'd try to work something out with him."

"Or her," added Kacey. "Wait, could people talk to sharks? Why didn't they ask Jaws to stop eating people?"

"Right, or her," said Rebecca. "No, people didn't figure out how to talk to sharks. But don't worry; I don't think there's anything out here. We've been traveling a long time and haven't found anything."

"How long?"

"Well, it's 2066, and Hugh and Arnold and Opal all left on 1977. So, that's, what?" Rebecca waited to see if the kids could do the math without writing it down.

"Almost one hundred years," said Kelvin.

"Eighty, no, wait," said Kacey, "eight-nine years.

Depending on what month it is, and what month they left Earth."

"Good!" said Rebecca. "If we haven't found anything in eighty-nine years, almost one hundred years," she added to reward Kelvin's quick approximation, "then there's probably nothing out here to threaten us."

"But we have a long way to go, don't we?" asked Kacey.

"Yep. It's possible we'll find something. But I think it would be more exciting than scary."

10—EARTH: THE BAINES FAMILY (2036, 2062, 2064): COMPILED FROM HOME-HOLOGRAM FOOTAGE

King and Baines didn't exactly become household names when their first article was published on November 17, 2014.

The piece—somewhat unoriginally titled "The Secret Manned-Voyager Flight of 1977" was the rare article about technology and space travel that was both accessible and enjoyable. At first, many readers only caught an abbreviated version of the story on the news or passed through it via a click-bait version in their social media feed. Their story about the secret Voyager 3 program did garner some attention, but most members of the media assumed it was a one-and-done story. A one-hit wonder, if you will.

Then, nine years later, the June 5, 2023 issue of *The New Yorker* was in the ether. This time the piece was nearly twice as long and more cleverly titled: "Just How Many Voyagers Were There?" The subheading was more in keeping with their first article title, "The Secret Second Manned-Voyager Program, Launched in 2001." Jackie wanted to publish again with *Discover* and was surprised that Troy felt strongly about going with *The New Yorker*.

"Why?" she asked.

"I love that magazine." It wasn't the strongest argument.

"Circulation-wise, I think *Discover* reaches more people. Plus, *Discover* fits the topic more thematically, and," she added quickly when she saw Troy's mouth begin to open and protest, "we'll have more freedom because we've already published there."

"There's no way *Discover* reaches more people than *The New Yorker*. You've got me on theme and consistency, but I don't know; this just feels like a bigger story. Plus, have you ever read the cartoons in *The New Yorker*?"

"Yes." Jackie rolled her eyes.

It wasn't that Jackie didn't "get" the jokes—she got the references, she understood the play on words, she saw what was supposed to be "funny"—they just didn't make her laugh. In all her sixty-four years, she had never once cut out a *New Yorker* cartoon to hang on the door of her office, nor had she ever forwarded any to a friend or shared one on any social media.

Troy, on the other hand, loved the cartoons. He subscribed to the magazine and always intended to read the whole issue but rarely did. He did, however, always read (and sometimes re-read and re-read again) the cartoons. Unlike Jackie, Troy did share the cartoons and cut them out to hang on his door. He liked how it made him feel smarter because not everyone understood the jokes.

Occasionally, just to amuse himself, Troy slipped the captions into conversation. If someone asked about the price of gasoline, Troy would quote Dator, saying, "It's $1.85 a gallon, and with every fill-up you get a free baby seal covered in oil." If Troy found himself at a barbecue, he might quote Noth: "How come when men cook outdoors it's 'barbecuing,' but when women do it it's 'witchcraft'?" Other times, he was happy to use a Noth line to break-up a serious conversation with something like, "Well, by that logic no one would ever shave a clock into a monkey." Or, if a friend asked, "What did I do wrong?" Troy might respond in Dator-fashion with, "They were fine with the tyranny, cruelty, and oppression, but you really pissed them off when you rooted for the wrong football team."

"Beyond my love of their cartoons, *The New Yorker* will allow us more space to really go deep," Troy chucked at his pun. "No seriously; they don't bat an eye at doing an article as long as 10,000 words—sometimes longer. Remember trying to whittle down the first piece to fit Discover's word count?"

That was a much stronger argument than Jackie had anticipated. She sighed. On occasion, she did read articles from *The New Yorker*, but often found them jargon-y, full of extraneous commas, and written in unnecessarily high-brow language that made reading the pieces a chore. After confirming that *The New Yorker* did in fact have a higher circulation than *Discover*—almost five times as much—she conceded.

"Just because I'm saying yes doesn't mean they'll take it," she said.

"I'm so excited!" Troy hugged her suddenly.

The article was accepted and published and well-received by readers and the media in general. Jackie and Troy did the media rounds. Their talks and the publicity around their events prompted the public to put pressure on NASA to reinvestigate the possibility of the Alcubierre warp drive. The hope was not only for a huge leap forward in space travel technology but also for the possibility of saving the crew from the earlier Voyager missions. Conspiracy theorists rose up and demanded to know what wasn't in their articles. Surely, there must be more. If NASA was willing to go on the record about Voyager 3 and 4, then there must be more they were not telling.

Jackie worked until she was seventy-three and then she finally retired. For once, she was able to do all the traveling she had always wanted to do. She polished off her list of states she'd never been to and visited all fifty. Then she visited the territories: Guam, American Samoa, Northern Mariana Islands, Puerto Rico, and the US Virgin Islands. She had just arrived in Puerto Rico when Troy's mother Louise died.

"I'm so sorry I can't be there for your family," she said.

"I only wanted you to know because I know you'd be hurt if I didn't include you," said Troy. "But please, enjoy your visit."

When Jackie had first started traveling, Troy referred to her excursions as trips or vacations, but Jackie corrected him.

"They're visits," she said. "Trips is too defined for what I'm doing. And vacations indicates you're getting away from something. I'm visiting. I'm learning. I'm not escaping anything, and I'm certainly not tripping around. They're visits of indeterminate length. Because, really, where else do I have to be?"

Jackie spent a week on each of ten Greek Isles, then another week in Vanuatu. Troy understood the desire to see the Greek Isles, but he had never even heard of Vanuatu. After doing some research about the country, he learned that most people went to Australia and then might stop off at Vanuatu for a side-trip, but it wasn't primarily a destination.

"Why Vanuatu?" he asked.

"It has a fun name to say," said Jackie. "I remember hearing it on the news in the 80s, something about some kind of rebellion then. But then there was this news piece about the Vanuatu singers, and their music is just amazing. And the water drumming. Wow. I want to see it."

"Water drumming?"

"See?" Jackie said, smiling at him. "It captures the imagination."

Everywhere she went, she sent messages back about her adventures. After Vanuatu, it seemed like Jackie took it as a personal challenge to find the most obscure places to visit (well, obscure anyway to Troy's Western sensibility).

"I didn't even know Macedonia was still a thing," Troy once said to Rose when a postcard arrived from Macedonia.

When the postcard arrived from Blagaj, Troy was convinced it was a typo. Other messages came from Turkmenistan, Mauritius, and Kyrgyzstan, and Seychelles, and Bhutan.

"Did you know, in Bhutan they measure their country's worth by the Gross Domestic Happiness instead of GDP?" Jackie's message asked, before explaining.

Even when Jackie visited places that were more common for tourism, she often went to the parts that were not well known or highly sought after as destinations. When she went to Japan, she visited Cat Island and Gokayama, not Tokyo or Kyoto. When she went to China, she visited Kunming and Honghe, not Shanghai or Beijing. When she went to India, she stayed in Assam and Nagaland and Manipur, not New Delhi or Mumbai.

"You know," Jackie said one night at the Baines's house, "space is amazing and all, but there's enough here on Earth to fill multiple life times."

This is how Troy liked to remember Jackie after she moved into a retirement community. As her memory faded, Troy or Rose or Harper or Junior would show Jackie photographs of things they had only experienced vicariously through her visits and relive the adventures she had once enjoyed. When she passed, at eighty-nine, Troy spoke at length at her wake. "She once said there was enough on Earth to explore to fill multiple life times, but she did her best to cover as much ground as possible. I'll miss my friend and collaborator, but I know she leaves this world with no regrets."

Harper also spoke briefly. "For me, Jackie was like another mother, and I know my own mother won't take any offense to that. She opened my eyes to so many things and was an amazing listener. I'm sure it's why my dad and she collaborated so well together. I'll miss her."

"People always ask me if I was ever jealous of the relationship my husband had with Jackie King," said Rose. "Jealous? I always said I'm glad he has someone to talk shop with so I can read my books." Heads nodded and there was a murmur of laughter. "The truth is, I was jealous of Jackie, but not because of that. It was because of the incredible woman she was and all that she accomplished in her life. We should all aspire to be more like Jackie King."

"I had the privilege of going with her on one of her visits," said Junior when it was his turn to speak. "Right out of high school, she took me to Assam. That's in Northeast India. I wanted to go to Europe, or Hawaii, but Jackie said since she was paying for it, I'd go where she wanted to go. And she wanted to go to Assam. I'd never heard of Assam before that trip and had no idea what to expect. What an eye-opening experience. I wouldn't have had it any other way. When I asked her later why she wanted to take me there, she went into this long discussion about empathy. I won't recount every point now, but I bet I could because it stuck with me, but here's the short version: You visit Europe to see the past of the Western world, but you visit anywhere else in the world, and you come away with an incredible sense of connectedness. You, and your little world is put into perspective. And she was absolutely right. As a gay man, I've been in the minority before, but never like this. Never so obviously. I could always 'pass' if I wanted. I have the privilege of whiteness, but in Assam that whiteness marked me. At eighteen, I probably didn't fully appreciate the lesson. But as I got older, traveled more, and lived more, I have appreciated it more and more every day. Thank you Jackie."

After the wake, Troy, Rose, and Harper joined Junior and his husband Clifton for dinner at his house. Troy and Junior immediately went to the grill to check on the ribs. They had started the charcoal early in the morning, and the ribs had been enjoying some indirect heat as they slowly cooked and waited for the grill masters to return. At thirty-seven, Grover was long past the point of needing his grandfather's help on the grill, but he had grown into a man who enjoyed having his help anyway. With the funeral fresh on his mind, Grover felt a need to be with his family even more than usual. Clifton brought beer and broke up the debate about if the ribs needed another coat of sauce or not.

"So, are we going to have brunch any time soon?" he asked. Clifton handed Grover one of the bottles in his hand. He clinked his bottle neck against Grover's.

"Brunch is more than just a time of day," Grover said. He winked at Clifton. "It's about a marriage of breakfast and lunch, not just about eating later in the day."

"Sorry, should I have asked about linner? Or dunch?"

"I don't like the sound of dunch," Troy said. "Can we just settle for the ribs will be done closer to two?"

"We used to call it supper," said Rose as she joined the party in the backyard.

"What about early dinner or late lunch?" asked Harper as she plucked at the deadheaded flowers in the garden. "Just call it like it is." She gave up the garden and walked over to her father. "So, Dad? What now? Are you going to pick up her traveling bug? Or publish another article?"

"Nah. Half of King and Baines is dead. What more do I have to say?" Troy looked to Rose. "But your mother and I have talked about traveling more, er, visiting," he winked at them. "Maybe not quite as adventurously as Jackie did. But more than we do now."

"Which won't be difficult to accomplish since we all we do now is really just scuttle back and forth between our house, yours, and Junior's," Rose said.

"What about me?" asked Clifton, mocking hurt.

Rose rolled her eyes.

"Your mother just rolled her eyes at me!" Clifton said.

"Certainly not. Eighty-three-year-old women do not roll their eyes; it's unbecoming," Rose said with mock indignation. "Oh, Cliffy; you know we love you."

Troy and Rose did travel more. Not nearly as widely or obscurely as Jackie had, but they saw much of the world. Most often they were alone in their travels, but sometimes Clifton and Grover joined them, and sometimes Harper did as well— though she was more of a homebody than a traveler. The shared travel experiences typically began with Rose and Troy arriving and the others joining sometime later (and then typically leaving before Rose and Troy did). One thing you could bank on was whenever it was cold, you would find Rose and Troy in the opposite hemisphere enjoying perpetually warm weather.

"My only bucket list item left to complete," Troy said to his grandson one day, "is to never be cold again."

"It's all in how you define 'cold,'" Clifton replied. "Cold is a state of mind."

"I don't know, fifty-four degrees is plenty cold," said Troy.

"What about ice skating? Or sledding?" Grover asked.

"I might make an exception now and then, particularly if great grandchildren are involved."

Eventually there would be great grandchildren, but by then Grover's family would live far enough south that there would never be any snow. It also ensured that the great grandparents wouldn't have any excuse not to be home for Christmas.

When they were at the ice rink a few days later, Grover helped his grandfather lace up his skates.

"Wouldn't it have been easier to go with the ones with the big clip across the front?" asked Troy.

Grover ignored the comment and said, "I remember you took me ice skating as a kid and how I could never get my laces tight enough." He pulled on the laces and grunted. "But you showed me this trick of pulling, and holding with your other finger, and then working your way all the way up the laces." Grover performed the actions as he spoke. "Until you're at the very top, and then you would tell me how your dad used to wrap the laces around the back of your ankles and how much you hated that."

"It wasn't safe!" Troy said.

"Yes, I remember you saying that you could break your ankle from the laces being that tight," said Grover. "And you told me how you used to tell your dad that, and he'd just say, well what am I supposed to do with all these laces?" Grover looked down at his hands and saw he was facing the same dilemma. "Which is a damn good question. Why do they make laces so long?" He tied the laces as best he could, extended the loops so that the loose laces didn't hang down, double-knotted them, then looked at his father. "How'd I do?"

Troy smiled, and then pushed off his grandson's shoulder to stand and waddled over to the other little ones. They too were standing on wobbly ankles.

"Are you sure it's safe?" Clifton asked his husband. "He's ninety-five, right?"

Grover shrugged. "Not until next month. Besides, people are living longer and longer all the time."

"You don't see your mom out here," said Clifton. "I'm just worried about him."

"He'll be fine."

Out on the ice, Troy was more than fine. Though he had grown up in Florida, his father was a native of northern Michigan and had made sure that Troy knew how to handle himself on a pair of ice skates. While Rose and Harper huddled under a space-heater hanging from the ceiling and his great grandchildren and grandchild clung to the walls for support, the ninety-five-old Troy amazed onlookers with his speed, ability, and showers of ice from his hockey-stops. The old man enjoyed himself and put on quite a show for a half hour or so. After that, he slowed and spent time teaching his great grandchildren. His old knees wouldn't have tolerated much more of the abuse. He enjoyed teaching his great grandchildren how to push and glide.

"Lyle," he said to his oldest great grandchild, "push, glide, feet together, push, glide."

Adrian, age eight, was a natural. Under her grandfather's tutelage she immediately grasped the basic concepts and was able to race around the rink and weave between the slower skaters. She even tried to help her fathers. They listened attentively but ultimately were content to hold hands and slowly walk on the ice rather than glide across it.

Later, Rose commented, "All these years of marriage, and I never knew you could do that."

"I'm a regular man of mystery," Troy said as he winked at her.

Two years later, on July 15, Troy was dead at the age of ninety-seven. On March 14, 2064, Rose followed him. While the family mourned each equally, only Troy's passing was newsworthy to the larger public. The family kept the service small, but Harper and Grover were both reached for comment by media outlets. Neither of them was prepared for how to deal with that kind of attention.

"I don't really have much to say," said Grover. "I mean, I loved my grandfather. He was a wonderful person."

"He was my dad," said Harper. "He did all kinds of things. Writing those two articles was just one thing he did, and it wasn't even that big of a deal to him."

With Troy's passing, both articles he and Jackie wrote re-emerged in the news cycle. People revisited the discussions of the Voyager 3 and 4 programs and again raised the question of why no attempt had been made to rescue the crews. When pressed, NASA officials said they had been working on the warp drive first proposed in 1994, but that they didn't have the time, money, or resources to make the strides necessary for such a rescue mission to be possible.

"Even without the warp drive, isn't our technology now faster and better than it was in 2001 when Voyager 77 went up?" asked a talking head on the news.

"Of course it is," responded a NASA official, "and that technology was better than the technology in 1977. But both of those missions have traveled so far, it would take decades, or centuries, to catch up with them. You have to remember, they had unique trajectories based on the line-up of planets that allowed them to benefit from gravitational assist. Even though those craft are slower than ours are now, it doesn't mean we'll be able to pop over and pick them up. We're simply not willing to risk the lives of more astronauts without more of a sure thing. A warp drive is the closest thing we could have to that sure thing."

Projections were made as to how many generations of astronauts might now be hurtling through space, and how feasible Dr. Alcubierre's warp drive would be. Those discussions and the attention brought by Troy's passing ultimately resulted in increased funding to NASA by the Federal government and then funding from the various billionaires who had become interested in space travel.

By the time Grover and Clifton were renewing their vows in 2075, NASA had announced it was ready to launch a rescue mission by 2077. Some speculated NASA was holding out for the anniversary of the first Voyager flight, but in reality, it was the year that planetary alignment would be ideal—or at least as good as it would get for the foreseeable future.

Grover and Clifton initially missed the announcement of the launch as they were busy celebrating their renewed vows and mingling with friends and relatives at a reception in their honor. The happy couple entered the reception and looked out at everyone gathered. They couldn't help but smile. Clifton kissed his husband and then walked away to the DJ booth. The DJ handed Clifton the microphone. Everything up to this point had been planned out, and now Grover wasn't sure what was happening. As much as Grover was excited to publicly express his love for Clifton and to celebrate thirty years of marriage, he wasn't overly fond of being the center of attention. But now here he was. Standing in front of nearly everyone he knew, as his husband prepared to do something that Grover was unprepared for. Grover assumed it would be some kind of toast, which shouldn't have surprised him because toasts happen at this sort of event, but he had assumed when toasts were given that he would be next to his husband and they would be shielded by the table, not exposed like this center stage.

"Thank you all for coming," Clifton started. "It's been an incredible thirty years that Grover and I have shared together, and there are many more years of wedded bliss to come." The people seated at the tables clapped and cheered. "But this year also marks another special occasion. I'm not sure how many of you know, but my dear, sweet, husband turned sixty-four about a month ago." Clifton turned from his audience to look directly at Grover. "I still have a year before I join you at this magical set of digits, but I hope when that time does come, that you'll still love me as much as I love you." Clifton turned back to the DJ and nodded, and then pivoted back to his spouse. "But I don't want to assume—you know, that whole ass-u-me thing—so I need to ask…"

And Paul McCartney took over as Clifton set down the microphone, walked to Grover, took his hand, and began their first dance.

That dance and the toast were the most talked about moments of the reception.

"You hold onto that one," said Heather from Grover's work.

"He's something special," her husband said as he gripped Grover's shoulder and smiled.

Great Aunt Cecilia shook Clifton's hand and stared into his eyes. Her lips parted as if to say something, but no words came. Eventually she let go and walked towards the door.

"I always thought that was a goofy song," said Clifton's friend Jason, "but, you might have changed my mind about it."

Their friends Ryan and Darrin gave each partner a hug. "That 'will you still feed me' line is going to become a painful reality before you know what hit you," Ryan said and laughed. But immediately behind him in line was Clifton's great Uncle Tyler in a wheelchair, being pushed by his wife Clara. Clifton followed his gaze and shrugged. He gave Ryan another hug before turning his attentions to Tyler and Clara.

Finally, Harper brought up the end of the line. "Hey you two." She hugged them both. "It was a great night. You put on a good show."

"Thanks Mom," said Grover.

"Someone taught him well," said Clifton.

"I got to talking with your friend Darrin," she said. "He's a nice guy. Did he tell you about the news?"

"Are they adopting another child?" asked Grover.

"They seem a bit old for that," said Clifton. He smiled and

laughed.

"No, about NASA," Harper said. "I haven't been following since your grandfather passed, but I guess they made a major announcement today." She paused. "Well, I guess a major announcement about an upcoming major announcement."

Grover raised his right eyebrow and waited.

"Two years and they think the warp drive thing will be ready to try to rescue the other Voyager crews. I guess it's working now, but the planets will be lined up better, and something about gravity boost, or assist, or something like that. And, of course, it's the one hundredth anniversary of the first Voyager."

"They're always big on round numbers and anniversaries," said Clifton. "But, that's pretty exciting."

"I hadn't heard at all," said Grover. His grandfather had passed on to him his love of space, and Grover had been following the space program, but today he had given the entirety of himself to simply being present and enjoying the day. "Have they received any signals from either 3 or 4? Do they have any idea if they're alive?"

"Sorry, I don't know anything else," Harper laughed.

"Wait, you said the warp drive is working? How many tests have they done? Where did they test it? And how?" Grover asked.

"Hon, you have the full extent of my knowledge at this point," Harper said. She laughed and looked at her son-in-law. "Sorry. I'm guessing he's going to be up late getting caught up now."

"Yeah, probably," said Clifton. "But it was a hell of a party today, wasn't it?" He hugged Harper again and wished her a good night.

Grover did stay up late reading multiple accounts and reactions to the announcement. There was no indication that NASA had made contact with Voyager 3 or 4, or that they had any idea if the crews were alive. The technology was simply something that had been in development since Dr. Harold Sonny White gave his speech in 2011, and the development of this technology was not created directly to aid or assist or rescue the Voyager crews, but rather now that they had the technology, it could be used for that purpose. The actual directive of what would simply be called Voyager (no number, though many would refer to it as Voyager 5), was to complete the mission that Voyager 3 was created to do—explore the Alpha Centauri system. This Voyager wouldn't be done in secret, and it wouldn't take millennia to accomplish the mission. Current projections were claiming that Voyager 5 would arrive in the Alpha Centauri system in 0.43 Earth years—nearly 157 days. This was a huge improvement over the 4.3 years it would have taken assuming NASA could create a spaceship capable of traveling the speed of light.

"They think they can get all the way to Alpha Centauri in less than half a year!" Grover told a mostly-sleeping Clifton. "That's crazy! So, they can definitely reach the other ships way before then. Because, they're like, what?" He did some calculations in his head and Clifton began to doze again.

"Well, it would have taken Voyager 3 some 40,000 years to get there."

Clifton stirred again and turned over.

"I think Jackie and Grandpa's paper said Voyager 3 was traveling 70,000 mph, so that's, like, 600-million miles in a year. And they've been traveling since 1977, so, 60-billion miles? Is that right?"

There was no answer.

"And Alpha Centauri is almost 26-trillion miles away. Huh. Anyway, it's way closer. They should be able to get the crews from both Voyager 3 and 4 without much time at all. Wow." Grover closed his eyes and tried to join his husband in sleep, but it took him a while before his mind finally shut off enough to let him.

Harper wouldn't live to see the launch of Voyager 5, but Clifton, Grover, and all the grandchildren would all be there.

11—SPACE, VOYAGER 3, 2076: TWO UNEXPECTED DEATHS

By 2076, as Voyager 3 was nearing its one hundredth year in space, two deaths shocked the crew members. By now there were ten people packed in the ship. Between those ten people, there was almost always at least one game of cards being played. It would be safe to say that there were easily between ten and twenty games played per day. Over nearly a century of play, the cards took a lot of abuse from the oils on the astronauts' fingers to the bending and flicking that occurred when picking at cards or placing them, and the shuffling that occurred at least once per game.

It was while Sidney was showing Kacey how to shuffle the deck of cards that the first of two deaths occurred. Instead of fitting neatly into one another and then allowing her to bridge the cards back together, the cards literally disintegrated in her hands. At first Kacey was amazed; she thought it was some kind of magic trick. One minute Sidney was manipulating the cards, and the next minute bits of paper were floating around in front of them.

"Wow!" Kacey said.

The older members of the crew immediately knew the death for what it was: The unavoidable end of entertainment on board the ship. The cards had probably been shuffled and dealt and played (conservatively) over 300,000 times, and some of the cards were dog-eared and flimsy. They hadn't foreseen the eventual disintegration of the deck, but they should have expected it at some point. Now they wondered how long it would be before their books crumbled from overuse and their music wore out.

The thought put everyone in a rather somber mood. This was made worse when Eva was found dead shortly after the deck of cards died. Eva wasn't the first human death on board the ship as Kirk, Amelia, and Edgar had all taken their lives decades ago, but this was the first natural death onboard. Everyone had assumed that since Hugh was still alive and kicking at one hundred and thirty-five, everyone would live a long life. Eva was only seventy-eight.

There were no obvious natural threats on board the ship. Occasionally tempers flared when a crew member got angry with another, but no one had ever turned violent. Everything that went in and out of the bodies of the astronauts was carefully controlled, so it wasn't like someone was going to slip some poison into someone's food. They weren't exposed to new germs or bacteria. Without the tug of gravity, the organs lasted longer. And yet, Eva's death made it clear that they had overlooked something.

Unfortunately, none of them was properly trained as a medical examiner.

They did the best they could, but there were no obvious signs of discomfort before she passed, and there were no obvious external signs of what might have caused her death. In fact, Sidney had just been with Eva prior to the death of the cards, and she had seemed fine.

"I mean, she was reading, which she loved to do, so I guess she was happy," Sidney said.

"What about something like sudden cardiac arrest?" asked Opal.

"A heart attack?" asked Hugh.

"No, that's different," said Opal. "With sudden cardiac arrest, it happens, as the name suggests, suddenly and without warning."

"Why?" asked Sidney. "What causes it?"

"I'm not sure we know, but it can be impacted by a family history of heart disease," said Opal.

"I'm sorry, but I'm confused," said Hugh. "How is it different from a heart attack?"

"A heart attack, generally, has warning signs. But it's almost always caused by a blockage in an artery," said Opal. "Sudden cardiac arrest happens suddenly and without warning. It's like the heart just malfunctions abruptly."

"Huh," said Sidney. "Well, Eva didn't appear to have any kind of distress earlier. But, then again, I wasn't with her right when it happened. And unfortunately, we don't know anything about her family history."

"That's not something I considered before," said Arnold. "I guess it would be helpful to know a little about family history for things like this."

"Or to avoid mixing genes that might produce unfavorable results," said Hugh.

"Part of why the eggs and sperm aren't identifiable is to prevent us from trying to control the gene pool," said Opal. "But I agree; this is one instance where it would be helpful to know a little about the samples we're pulling from."

"That does it for both of the nineties babies then," said Rebecca rather coldly. Before anyone could ask for clarification, she added, "Both Eva and Edgar are gone now, 1998 and 1999. A whole generation is missing."

"What about me?" asked Amber. "I was born in 2000, so I'm not a 90s baby, but they were definitely my generation."

"Oh, sorry," said Rebecca. She hugged Amber.

Eva's body was stripped of clothing in order to conserve what little supplies they had, and Opal stepped into the airlock with her. She clipped herself in and then opened the airlock to space and gently pushed Eva outside of Voyager 3. From inside, the crew watched as Eva floated away from the ship and disappeared into the darkness.

12—HOW THINGS MIGHT HAVE GONE, BUT DIDN'T

In another version of this story, Voyager 3 and 4 might both have been allowed to complete their journeys without interruption. They would have chugged along at their respective speeds, gone through the various generations of crew, struggled for—literarily—thousands of years, and would one day finally land on the planet they originally sought. What would they have seen when they landed? Voyager 4 would have gotten there much sooner than the flight that departed in 1977, but long after Voyager 5 made it there.

Voyager 4 would arrive in 21238 and would find an American flag and some evidence of space junk left behind by Voyager 5.

The first sign that someone was there before them would be the space junk orbiting the planet. It that might have been read as a hopeful sign and a sign of life. When they landed, they'd see the flag, and the obvious signs of short-lived habitation. What would they do next?

In any scenario, they would step out of the spaceship and explore. That's what explorers do. Can they walk here? None of the crew has ever experienced planetary-gravity in this way. What will happen to their organs when there is suddenly a gravitational pull? Even if they are able to walk around normally without ill effects, what then? Do they stay and try to create a new civilization as originally planned? Their ship was designed to perpetuate food and water from waste, so it's possible they could live here for as many generations as they are willing to stick it out. Do they try to fly back home?

There are several problems with trying to return to Earth. First, it is very unlikely they have enough fuel to launch. The ship was not designed to make a return trip. Second, what if there is no Earth left to return to? A lot has happened in the previous nineteen thousand years. Third, define "home." None of this crew has ever known a home aside from space and this ship. Even if they did want to return to Earth, it is unlikely the Earth they'd be returning to would be recognizable by even the original crew, much less the version of Earth created in the minds of the current crew based on the stories they were told.

So, maybe they stay? Maybe they stay, live long lives, but choose not to procreate. Maybe they do try to launch and fail. Maybe, through some miracle, they succeed in their launch attempt and end up passing Voyager 3 a second time—thus lapping that ship; how tragic would that be? And, maybe, just maybe, they do figure out a way to eek out survival on this foreign land.

Now for Voyager 3. Let's just assume for a moment they make it, arriving in 43200. It's a very, very, very unlikely scenario, because it assumes that their food or supplies didn't run out, and that their ship didn't suffer unrepairable damage, and that the crew didn't suffer extreme radiation levels rendering them unable to reproduce, and that the crew simply didn't go bat-shit crazy from the confinement and boredom of the centuries of limited access to privacy or exercise or scenery. But, let's assume they land. And let's assume they still had functioning spacesuits. And let's assume the knowledge from each generation was successfully conveyed to the next so that there is no mistake made when they exit the airlock and step onto a foreign planet. Remember, this will be the very first planet any of them have stepped onto, as none of them have ever known anything other than life inside the capsule. But, for the sake of this story, at least one astronaut steps onto the planet. What does he or she see?

There is an American flag. There is space junk.

Maybe Voyager 4 is there. If Voyager 4 is there, maybe it's abandoned. Or maybe the Voyager 4 crew managed to create a settlement. Or maybe Voyager 4 holds the remains of its long dead crew. Or maybe Voyager 4 isn't there. If it's not there, then the Voyager 3 crew might wonder what happened to that spaceship that they heard legends of that passed them back in 2022? But, eventually, the Voyager 3 crewmember would shake that thought off and address more pressing concerns.

How does this crewmember know if he or she can remove his or her helmet? The crew from Voyager 4 would have been better prepared because they would have had more gauges and tools, but Voyager 3 was put together on a shoestring budget. Do they have a gauge to measure the atmosphere? Or, will it just require one brave soul to test it out and see what happens? If someone's going to test the air, do they draw straws for it? Does someone willingly say they're willing to risk his or her life for that opportunity? Maybe they opt for the oldest member of the crew? Or the one that's seeking to end his or her life? It's really hard to say.

Once they know if the air is safe to breathe or not, then they face all the same problems Voyager 4 faced. Except, return is not even remotely in the cards for them. There's no way the old bucket of bolts can launch again. Whatever fuel it has, after nearly forty-two thousand years in space, is nowhere near what they need to lift it off the ground. So, their choices are limited to: 1) continuing to live on board the spaceship, as they've existed for thousands of years, 2) "opt out," or 3) try their luck on this planet. They have plenty of eggs and sperm waiting to create more astronauts, but that will take time. And gravity is going to be an issue (so will walking or any means of locomotion). If the air is breathable, then it will make life a lot easier. Maybe they'll find resources on the planet that make it habitable.

That would be a hopeful ending.

More realistically, they wouldn't have made it here in the first place because one of the following would happen:

Hit by space debris—man-made or otherwise.

Ran out of food.

Ran out of energy.

Radiation levels prevented procreation.

Radiation levels caused death.

Information was not successfully conveyed from one generation to the next resulting in a catastrophic failure.

Ran out of oxygen.

Carbon dioxide was not successfully eliminated.

After many, many years of disuse the spacesuits deteriorated, rending them useless.

A contagious disease or illness kills the crew.

Something unexpected happens with the bacteria inside our body.

Or any number of other scenarios we haven't considered.

But of all of those possibilities, wouldn't it be most tragic if they did make it and crashed while trying to land? After all those years of defying the odds? Maybe they are looking backwards into space as they try to bring the ship down. They can't see Earth now, but it's there winking back at them. Hell, if humans are still able to survive on Earth at this point, they might very well be looking at the Alpha Centauri System, too. And maybe one of the crew is, unbeknownst to him or her, having a staring contest with someone light years away. Maybe that person on Earth manages to see a blip as Voyager 3 disappears from existence due to any number of navigational mistakes.

One of these, or a combination of these, sad or potentially lonely endings for Voyager 3 and/or 4 might have come to pass, if not for the curiosity of that young boy back in 1977. That curiosity sparked a casual investigation by that young boy's father, which in turn resulted in a folder of documents being stashed away in the attic for years until the daughter of the young boy, and the granddaughter of the father, arrived digging through the forgotten items looking to reclaim toys of her youth. Because of this chain of events an FOIA request was filed, the secrets of Voyager 3, and later 4, were unearthed, and when Voyager 5 finally flew (or worm-holed, or whatever the verb for its type of travel should be), it was able to rescue the crew of those otherwise forgotten, neglected spaceships.

Let's not worry about what if, we're in the home stretch now. Let's focus on what did.

13—EARTH: LAUNCH OF VOYAGER 5, SEPTEMBER 2077

It's safe to say that more people witnessed the Voyager 5 launch than anyone else in the history of space launches. Even adjusted for population increases, the physical audience for the launch and the combined live-streaming audience dwarfed anything that came before it. People swarmed to Florida to be present for the historic event, and many of them also live-streamed it so they had a better view of what was going on close-up. Bars were full with all the patrons focused on the screens that were tuned to the launch.

The ship itself was a sight to behold. It was the single largest, most massive (literally) craft to be launched from Earth. The previous record was held by STS-117 (Shuttle Atlantis), weighing in at 270,470 pounds and operating between 1985 and 2011. The Atlantis was "only" 1,881 pounds heavier than its companion, Endeavour, but it was enough to tip the scales in Atlantis' favor as the record holder. However, at 517,228 pounds, Voyager 5 beat the record for heaviest craft launched by 246,758 pounds.

The reporters busily rattled off all the statistics and measurements about the craft, before moving to biographies of the crew.

"Just who is on board?" they asked, though by this point the audience knew. The two men and two women who were risking their lives for this rescue mission were already household names throughout the world.

Eloise Fisher, 35, the captain of the crew, was born in Texas near Johnson Space Center where her parents both worked. As a toddler she wandered the halls and became something of a mascot to the workers. It was no surprise that she grew up to be an astronaut. Before she joined NASA, she had already captured America's heart as the first female quarterback to take the Houston Cougars to the Rose Bowl before winning the National Championship. She was a champion for women and young girls everywhere, and she was a powerful symbol of the old saying, "You can do anything you put your mind to." Yes, many women had broken down barriers before her to make this possible, and her family was wealthy enough to afford her the luxury of choosing a university of her preference, but somehow, despite all her silver-spoon-type privilege, Eloise was loved by rich and poor alike.

Eloise Fisher was a stark contrast from the criteria used to choose the captains of Voyager 3 and 4 who were both chosen for their ghost-like presence in the world. Eloise was the rising tide that lifted all ships. There was a lot of curiosity in whether the crews of Voyager 3 and 4 were alive, and if they were, how they would fare back on Earth. People wondered if such a rescue was possible or even advisable. Would the crews want to come back to Earth? Would they be upset about having their missions interrupted? This curiosity and the wow-factor of Eloise garnered worldwide attention in the mission of Voyager 5.

If Eloise was the charismatic frontperson, then Ji Hennessey (28) and Yong Liscomb (31) were right behind her. Ji, the youngest of the crew, was the most involved directly in the engineering of Voyager 5. She was the most familiar with the inner workings and had made several notable suggestions for improvements to NASA before the flight.

Yong was a master mathematician, which might not seem like a selling point for children everywhere, but he quickly became a superhero in the minds of K-12 educators everywhere. Yong even wore a cape to one school appearance where he talked about the power of numbers, and immediately after his likeness was featured in educational posters.

"With math," Yong said, raising his fist into the air on the poster and in videos, "all things are possible. Math *is* understanding." All of the astronauts were gifted in math and engineering, but only Yong had made it his true passion.

Last, but not least, was Jose Mason (31). It wouldn't be fair to call him the Ringo of the band, because it wasn't that Jose was shy or goofy or generally overlooked the way Ringo had been with the Beatles. And that's not to say that Ringo is bad, or the lesser of the Beatles—even though it was commonly reported that John snidely once said, "Ringo isn't even the best drummer in the Beatles" (he never said such a thing)—it's just that, like Ringo, Jose held down the backbeat of the band. He was so efficient at what he did, which was a little of everything, that it was easy to forget he was there. Like Yong, Jose did the school circuit to meet school children and to motivate them, but, unlike Yong's visits, Jose's meetings were typically unannounced and more of a one-on-one experience. Jose worked best in small groups, not big crowds. He made a big impression on those he met with, but he didn't have the same charisma as the other three members of the Voyager 5 crew.

Voyager 5 was originally scheduled to launch on August 7, but a surprise storm made the weather conditions unfavorable, which pushed the launch date back to September 11, 2077. When the media reported on the new launch date, much was made about how it was the anniversary of the terrorist attacks and a show of defiance in the face of the enemy. Since it was the 76th anniversary of the attacks on the World Trade Center in New York, many viewers had to be reminded of what had occurred so long ago. But those who studied history knew that

September 11 was a date that simply, inexplicably, kept popping up over time. With only 365.2422 days in a year, there would be certain dates where "a lot of history happened" (as one newscaster was heard to say), but September 11 defied that logic.

History had a way of happening on this day, for good or for ill. It was the date that the Battle of Teutoburg Forest ended (in 9 CE). And when Charles the Great crowned Louis I Emperor (813 CE). It was when Andronicus I Komnenos was deposed and Isaac was placed on the throne of the Byzantine Empire (1185 CE). It was also the first recorded instance of perpetual Eucharistic adoration outside of Catholic Mass (1226 CE). William Wallace defeated the English on this day in 1297 CE. The five-day siege of Vilnius occurred during Lithuanian Civil War (1390 CE). Also, the Ottoman forces retreated from Malta (1565 CE).

It was on September 11 that Manhattan Island was "discovered" by Henry Hudson (1609 CE). The Siege of Drogheda ended with Oliver Cromwell's victory (1649 CE). Other war-related events occurred in 1683, 1697, 1708, 1709, 1714, 1758, 1775, 1776, 1777, 1780, and 1786. On September 11, 1789, Alexander Hamilton became the first Secretary Treasury of the United States. The Hope Diamond, and French crown jewels, were stolen on that day in 1792.

More war-related events occurred in 1800, 1802, 1803, 1813, and 1814. A former Free Mason was arrested on September 11, 1826, after he claimed he was going to publish the secrets of the organization, and then after his arrest he mysteriously disappeared. Four years later, the Anti-Masonic Party convention occurred on September 11. The Revolution of September 11 occurred in Buenos Aires, and they declared their independence as a Republic, in 1852.

Plenty of other notable war-related events occurred around the world on this date. In 1941, on September 11, Charles Lindbergh gave his Des Moines Speech in an attempt to persuade the American public to reject FDR's intention of entering World War II. Nine years later, on this date that Harry

Truman approved military operations north of the 38th parallel. In 1954, Hurricane Edna devastated New England. In 1961, Hurricane Carla became the second most powerful storm to ever to hit Texas.

Planes crashed in 1968 and 1974 on September 11. Pinochet seized dictatorial control of Chile in 1973 on September 11, and remained in power until 1990. On this day, in 1985, Pete Rose surpassed Ty Cobb's record for most career hits. In 1997, NASA's Mars Global Surveyor reached Mars. In 2005, Israel completed the disengagement plan. On September 11, 2007, Russia tested the 15,650 pound "father of all bombs," which detonated with the equivalent of 44 tons of TNT. In 2012, 315 people were killed in clothing factories in Pakistan. In 2015, a crane collapsed on a mosque in Saudi Arabia, killing 111 and injuring 394 more.

And on, and on, and on, and on. So, to say that Voyager 5 left Earth on September 11 because of some tribute to the Twin Tower attacks of 2001 is also to say it left Earth on that date as a tribute to all those other events that just so happened to occur on that date. There was something about September 11 that seems to cause events (rather than just demark them), and Voyager 5 was simply another one of those events.

Had the flight occurred on August 7, Harper Baines would have survived to see it, but just barely. She died two days later on August 9. Grover, Clifton, Lyle, and Adrian were all there with her on the 7th to watch the launch, but then it was scrapped. Instead, an impromptu barbeque was thrown. The kids, now 27 and 25, ran to their respective apartments to grab a few things, and Clifton went out to get more Marzetti's dressing for the coleslaw. Grover and his mother stayed behind and patiently waited for the others to return to start the party.

"Do you think they'll do it?" Harper asked.

"The chances look good," said Grover. "They've done all the tests, and really there was only one issue. But that was a year ago, and they've had plenty of time to fix that."

"I think it will work," she said.

"Me, too."

"Come here," Harper said.

Her son came closer. He wasn't sure what she wanted. She reached forward, brushed back her son's hair, ran a finger across his forehead, and abruptly plucked an eyebrow from his head.

"Ow!"

"It was an angry one," Harper said. "It had to go."

When it was time to leave, the last words Grover said to his mother were, "I love you," and "Adrian will come and check on you on Monday." Then he turned to his daughter and said, "Right? Monday?"

Adrian confirmed. Grover gave Harper a hug and repeated his love for her. Two days later, Adrian found her grandmother already dead, crumpled on the floor. Calls were made and everyone reconvened at the hospital. Arrangements were made, and they all said a final goodbye a week before Voyager 5 finally took to the sky.

On the day of the launch, the four crew members seemed completely dwarfed by the size of Voyager 5. Originally, NASA had planned on sending the parts of Voyager 5 into space to be assembled but decided instead to construct it on Earth for the security of being able to check and recheck and recheck it. So, here it was. Massive. It would launch, orbit Earth until it had the correct trajectory, and then do its thing.

Everyone waited.

Cameras zoomed in and out to remind viewers of the sheer scope of the craft about to launch. When cameras were focused on the crew, or workers, or mission control, it was easy to forget the scope of the mission. People on the ground who were within a three-mile radius were advised to wear ear protection. Most looked through binoculars or stared at live streams for better views leading up to the launch. When the countdown began, everyone turned to the ship to witness the historic launch with their own eyes.

Despite the work of King and Baines and similar work inspired by their investigative writing, there was plenty of

NASA's history that was relatively unknown. For example: Project Orion. Previous to Longshot, Daedalus, and Voyager 3, Project Orion was thought to be the answer to traversing the great distances of the universe. The first mentions of the project occurred in 1946 when calculations were made that suggested using a nuclear propulsion system, but it didn't get underway until 1968. The basic idea was to have "nuclear pulse units" fired out the back of the craft; by "nuclear pulse units" they meant atomic bombs with roughly the force of the ones dropped on Japan in World War 2. How many bombs? There were multiple proposals calling for any number between 540 and 1,000 "pulse units." It was calculated that the shockwaves from the explosions would propel the ship into space at an incredible speed; this seemed logical, but obviously was very dangerous. Ignoring the possible danger, calculations suggested such a craft could arrive at Alpha Centauri in as many as 1,330 years and as few as 133—depending on how many bombs they were willing to "pulse" out the back.

Surprisingly enough, danger to human life and nuclear fallout was not the reason NASA shelved the project. Instead, the nails in Project Orion's coffin were three-fold. First, the 1963 Partial Test Ban Treaty was signed, which attempted to put an end to the testing of thermonuclear weapons. Second, NASA wanted to focus on landing on the moon. Third, and perhaps most damning, was NASA lacked conviction in the value of a mission to such a distant location. "Let's explore what's around us first," was the common refrain.

None of this surfaced or was discussed during the coverage for the 2077 launch of Voyager 5. Instead, attention bounced between exteriors of the Voyager 5 craft, the interiors of the control room, and biographical pieces and footage of the crew members in classrooms and at interviews. Grover, Clifton, Lyle, and Adrian grew impatient with the incessant loop of footage.

"I wish they'd just get on with it," grumbled Adrian. "What's taking so long?"

"Didn't you hear the guy?" asked Lyle. He adopted the

announcer-type voice of one of the newscasters. "There are many moving parts here, and NASA just wants to make sure everything is in its place before it hits go."

"They don't just hit 'go'," Adrian said and snorted. "Do they think we're idiots?"

"Everything was ready to 'go' when Grandma was still alive; what's changed now?" asked Lyle.

"No one says you have to watch this," said Grover. "I'm happy watching the sky and waiting patiently."

"How very Zen of you," said Clifton, but he was doing the same. Both men were sitting in lawn chairs, reclined slightly, with their eyes partially closed.

"Well, it's not like you're going to miss it," said Grover. "You'll hear this all across Florida, even with the best earplugs and headphones in place."

"Headphones," said Lyle, laughing. "They don't make headphones anymore, Dad. I think you mean, ear protection."

"Or, hearing protection," said Adrian.

"Ear muffs?" offered Clifton.

"That's more of a winter thing," said Adrian.

"Oh, right. Hearing protection and ear protection sounds so formal though," said Clifton.

"Formal is, 'sound suppression device' or something like that," said Grover. "But the point is, you're not going to miss it. We're only six miles away. It will be loud."

"Well, it's not like the Krakatoa eruption," said Adrian. "That was loud."

"That's the loudest sound ever recorded," said Lyle. "No, it's not going to be that loud."

"Look, you don't need to be able to hear this thing 3,000 miles away," said Grover. "My point is—"

"Yes, yes, your point is that we don't have to keep looking at the screen to wait for the moment of launch," said Lyle. He realized his comment was a bit snarkier than he intended, and walked over to give Grover a hug to soften the blow.

"Countdown!" said Adrian.

And there it was. They could hear the neighbors all around

them counting.

"Ear protection!" Clifton yelled, and then looked around. Everyone had theirs on except for him. He slid his into place.

10.

9.

8.

7.

6.

5.

4.

3.

2.

1.

Liftoff.

Despite the warnings issued by NASA and the Federal government, many people wanted to be as close to the launch as possible. It wouldn't rupture the eardrums of people forty-four miles away like Krakatoa did, but the sound was sure to be damaging if not taken seriously. NASA wasn't 100% certain how loud it would be but definitely louder than any other previous launch. In the end, it was three miles. That was the distance decided upon by "officials," and they stood by that number. Despite three being the official number—maybe because it sounded good and was a nice round number and was easily accomplished and discouraged observers from stepping foot on NASA property—officials and media members encouraged people to be "ten miles or more away, just to be safe."

Since people barely wanted to adhere to the official three-mile suggestion, you can guess how many listened to the unofficial suggestion of ten miles. This really was a bit silly. Whether you're three miles away or ten miles away from something, you're going to have relatively the same view. You will still require binoculars, or telescopes, or, and this was the case of almost everyone, a screen to show you the close-ups that you couldn't see even if you were in one of the buildings at NASA. Even the NASA workers on site were staring at screens instead of poking their heads out of windows. Ultimately, most people stayed glued to their screens until they heard liftoff and then turned their faces to the sky to see Voyager take to the air with their very own eyes. It was a miraculous sight. People all across the state of Florida looked up and saw the spacecraft arch through the clouds and disappear into space.

Unfortunately, almost anyone viewing the launch outdoors at the clearly defined, officially stated, three-mile radius suffered a ruptured eardrum. As you might suspect, this severely hampered their enjoyment of the launch. Some people even up to five miles from the launch suffered the same fate. Consequently, the doctors' offices, urgent cares, and emergency rooms were overflowing with patients. It didn't take long for nurses to triage the situation and inform those in the crowded waiting rooms that there really wasn't much to do other than for them to wait.

"The vast majority of all ruptured eardrums," the common refrain went, "will heal within three months. We can prescribe an antibiotic to prevent an ear infection from occurring, but there is little else we can do."

Patients who demanded to see a doctor were met with tired physicians who barely bothered using their otoscopes to diagnose them. Instead, doctors wearily inquired of patients at the start of the visit, "So, how far were you from the launch?" If the answer was less than five miles, they broke the news to their patients with further ado.

A class action lawsuit was levied against NASA and the Federal government for negligence, but ultimately after almost a year in the court system, a judge ruled the Federal, "suggestion of ten or more miles" was a sufficient warning and dismissed the case. An appeal was attempted, but by then the members of the class action had functioning eardrums, and the class action lost members and momentum.

14—THE VOYAGER CREWS RETURN TO EARTH, 2077

Earth is 4.3 light years from the Alpha Centauri system. Or 4,068,120,000,000,000,000 kilometers from Earth. If for some reason you're still on the Imperial System, that's 25,278,120,000,000,000,000 miles. More commonly, the distance is 271,937 astronomical units. AUs, as they're abbreviated, are the mean distance from the center of the Earth to the center of the Sun. This is roughly 149.6 million kilometers. Measuring the galaxy and universe by units based on the distance between the Earth and Sun has been common practice since Archimedes, but it was only in 1976 that the unit was more precisely measured, then fine-tuned in 1983, adjusted in 2006, and finally in 2012 set to the value we have used since.

Voyager 5 didn't have to travel that far though because Voyagers 3 and 4 had barely dented the distance to the Alpha Centauri system over the one hundred years and seventy-six years they'd been traveling, respectively. Voyager 4 was further along due to the technological breakthroughs onboard owing to its later launch, but it still had generations to go before it would ever cross into the Alpha Centauri system.

When the new technology powering Voyager 5 was first introduced, the laypeople assumed the spacecraft's "warp" would be nearly instantaneous. It might have worked well for media-creators who didn't want to waste the viewer's time with the travel that occurred during the "warp," but in reality, it was a slower process. Even the Voyager 5 crew who knew what to expect were disappointed by how long it took.

They patiently reminded one another, "Voyager 3 has been out there for a hundred years; this is nothing."

The crew of Voyager 5 was accustomed to things happening, "Now, now," as Yong Lipscomb aptly noted. The tedious 3.804914 days it took Voyager 5 to catch up with Voyager 3 felt long and interminable.

"Hey," Eloise Fisher reminded everyone at a low point in morale, "remember, this is a drop in the bucket compared to our mission to the Alpha Centauri system. If you can't hack this, then you're definitely not going to be able to handle the four years it takes for the real mission."

To the crewmembers of Voyager 3, Voyager 5 appeared in an instant. This was completely different from 2022 when Voyager 4 passed Voyager 3. There was no gradual coming into view to give the crew in Voyager 3 time to realize what was happening. Voyager 5 just appeared. One moment there was nothing but the usual blackness and stars, and the next someone was tapping on the exterior of the spacecraft.

"Did you hear that?" asked Opal.

"Yes," said Hugh incredulously.

Kacey suited up and was the one who greeted Eloise from Voyager 5. The rest of the Voyager 3 crew huddled around as near to the airlock as possible. Improbably, there was another human in a space suit requesting to enter their craft. The suit was slimmer and obviously more maneuverable than their own, but it was clearly a spacesuit, and the person within it was definitely human. Kacey opened the airlock, Eloise floated in, and the two stood there staring at one another determining how best to proceed.

Once the shock of seeing another human in their quarters lessened, the Voyager 3 crew turned its attention to the spacecraft itself. Voyager 5 was massive. They had been living on a craft that was barely 35,000-pounds for the last one hundred years, and now here was a craft easily ten, maybe fifteen, times the size. Everyone marveled at its size and the beauty of its design.

"We're here to rescue you," Eloise finally said with authority and conviction.

"We haven't finished our mission," replied Hugh, still clearly shocked at the turn of events happening before his eyes.

Eloise looked at Hugh and saw a tired old man. She could tell he was stubborn, but it was unlikely that he was stupid. "You must have done the math by now." Eloise looked at the crew around her. "Conservatively, your course would take you forty-thousand, forty-one thousand years. What you did was brave, but in the end futile. This thing," she glanced around at Voyager 3, "might last that long, but none of you will. It was an exciting experiment, but we now have technology to get to the Alpha Centauri system in four years." She let that sink in.

"Can we go on that mission?" asked Kacey.

"That seems like a nice way to let us complete our original directive," Opal offered.

Eloise was careful in choosing her next words. "It's not up to me. NASA will have the final say. My mission is just to retrieve this crew and the crew of Voyager 4 and return to Earth."

Hugh visibly withdrew with a shudder. "There's no way NASA will ever let us fly again. They'll want to experiment with us, and see how our bodies adapted, and you," he pointed at the crew born in space, "They'll really want to study you."

"He's not wrong," Arnold Paul added. "But this is barely a life. Certainly not what I expected."

"I won't force you to come," said Eloise, "but I think you might be interested to see Voyager 5 and learn about what's happened in your absence. My crew and I can offer that to you."

"What about my ship?" asked Hugh.

"It will continue on," said Eloise. "Your ship is not part of my mission, but it might be part of someone's else's mission later. I'm just here for you and your crew."

Hugh was the last one to leave Voyager 3, and for a couple minutes it seemed like he might stay with the ship. "What do I have on Earth?" he kept asking. "I'm one hundred and thirty-six. How many more years do I have there?" He sighed again and again. "Hell, I've lived more of my life in space than I ever did on Earth," he said. "And not even just a little, but more like almost four times as much of my life was here in space."

No one refuted him or argued; they just waited patiently as he sorted his thoughts and made the decision himself. Finally, Eloise reached her hand out for him and, after a short hesitation, he reached back.

"Voyager 3," Eloise said. "Meet Voyager 5." She gestured grandly at the crew waiting for them on Voyager 5. Ji Hennessey, Yong Lipscomb, and Jose Mason all nodded while Arnold Paul, Opal Watts, Rebecca, Sidney, Amber, and Maggie entered the massive ship. The crew of Voyager 3 found plenty of room on board to stretch out and find their own corners to enjoy alone time in a way they hadn't been able to in almost a century (or, in the case of a few of them, ever). Once everyone was sorted, Eloise announced she was preparing to intercept Voyager 4.

"It will take another, 2.5 days," she said. "Give or take."

"And then Earth?" asked Sidney.

"Right," Jose said. "Then back to Earth. That will take," he ran the numbers in his head, "6.2 days, or so."

"Wow," Arnold said. "It seems unreal. Never thought I'd see home again. Honestly, didn't really care about ever seeing it again, but now that it's going to be a reality, I'm weirdly excited. What about you, Opal?"

Opal shrugged. "There will be a lot to catch-up on. I'm guessing most of the people we know will be dead. And I hate to admit that Hugh's right, but I'm guessing we'll be guinea pigs for quite a while."

Arnold nodded. "Sure, but eating anything other than a reconstituted protein-injected shit-burger sounds amazing."

"Assuming your gut can handle it," said Hugh.

"Party pooper," Opal said.

While the original Voyager 3 crew marveled at the possibilities of returning to Earth, Sidney, Rebecca, Amber, and Maggie were suspiciously silent, but their quiet went unnoticed amid the chatter of their Earth-born counterparts.

An empty Voyager 3 was left to continue on its way and a few days later, the whole experience was repeated with Voyager 4. This time Eloise found no resistance from the commander about abandoning their ship. While the atmosphere within Voyager 3 hadn't precisely been boisterous or jovial, it was in comparison to what Eloise found aboard Voyager 1. Voyager 1 hadn't lost a single crew member (to suicide or natural causes), but there was an air of defeat in the spacecraft. There was no chatter, no sense of camaraderie, no hint of this being a unit or team. Instead, it felt as though ten people had simply been cohabitating for the duration, almost entirely independent of one another. When Eloise said, "Hello! I've been sent to rescue you," she was met with ten shrugs and an overall attitude that could best be described as indifferent.

On board Voyager 5, the crew of Voyager 4 nodded to the Voyager 3 crew the way someone might nod to a driver of a similar make and model of car. Outwardly, the nod was simply one of acknowledgement; it said, "Hey, I see you. Do you see me?" but silently it conveyed a sense of shared experience. The Voyager 4 crew didn't look back at their old craft as it drifted away or mix and mingle much with the new humans. They took to their new quarters and remained mostly secluded for the duration of the trip home.

When Voyager 5 began orbiting Earth in preparation to land, all the crew members emerged to take in the view. There wasn't much conversation, but there was definitely a collective sense of awe. It had been one hundred years since Voyager 3 had left the Earth, and almost as long since Earth disappeared from their astral view, and seventy-six years since Voyager 4 had left. No vocalized "wows" were heard, but it was definitely implied.

The crew members who had been born in space and had

never seen Earth—outside of images—took it all in. Instead of barreling through darkness, they were circling this globe of blues and greens. Finally, Omar, the youngest of anyone on board at the age of seven, broke the silence and asked a question that most of the space-born crew were wondering, "What will I do when we land?"

"What do you mean?" asked Hugh.

"You'll be a hero," said Zach.

"What's a hero?" asked Joanna. "And will I be one, too?"

"A hero is someone who does something heroic," Zina said. "But now I'm guessing your next question is what heroic is. And that's harder to define."

"A hero, or someone that's heroic, does something for the greater good and puts themselves second," Nelda said.

"Or puts themselves at risk," said Opal.

"Why would I be a hero?" asked Omar. "I was just born here; I didn't make the choice to put myself at risk."

No one immediately answered.

Then Opal did, "Even still, to the people on Earth, you did something that few of them would have done."

"One time my friend and I were talking," Nelda said, "and he was arguing that firefighters weren't heroes. They were just people doing their jobs. Their job was a risky one, but it was still just their job. I guess my dad was listening, because all of the sudden he asked, are you a fireman? My friend shook his head. Are you going to be one when you grow up? My friend shook his head again. And my dad said, and I'm guessing that's because you're not willing to take the risks that they are. Right? They're heroes, plain and simple. Yes, it's their job, but they chose that career out of all the other possibilities."

Though she meant well, Nelda realized the mistake just as the words were tumbling out of her mouth.

"But we didn't choose," said Joanna quietly.

"It doesn't matter," said Arnold. "You'll still be heroes. What will you do? We'll probably never have to work another day of our lives because NASA will take care of us."

"What's it like to have a job?" asked Amber. "Could I have

one if I wanted to?"

Opal debated about how to answer the question and hoped that someone else would do it for her. Technically Amber, and Maggie, Rebecca, Sidney, Mabel, Bonnie, Salvador, Joanna, and Omar could all get jobs, but they had no relatable experience, other than being part of a multigenerational spaceship. Even on board they had few responsibilities. They lacked the diplomas and degrees that were the basic qualifications for nearly every job she could think of. Plus, several of them were past retirement; would they qualify for social security? Had they been collecting some kind of salary all these years? How would they care for themselves? She hoped that Arnold was right and that NASA would simply take care of them all. That was the right thing to do, but the government didn't always do the right thing.

"We're going to begin our descent now," Eloise announced and saved them all from making promises they couldn't keep.

Hugh Sullivan died almost immediately. The tug on his one-hundred thirty-six-year-old organs was too much.

Zach Sheridan went into cardiac arrest upon landing. At one-hundred-eleven, he was a spring-chicken compared to Arnold Paul or Opal Watts, but his body couldn't handle the sudden change. The crew scrambled to revive him, but he died before Voyager 5 came to a complete stop on the runway.

The others survived but immediately felt the effects of being in gravity. They were all rushed to special treatment centers and isolated from the press.

Reporters and camera crew were waiting for the Voyager 5 to disembark its human cargo. The world had continued to follow the great rescue mission and wanted to see the crews from the earlier Voyager missions. NASA shielded the ship from the media and only later did a brief press conference to confirm the safe arrival and success of the mission.

Reporter Yasmin Torres asked, "What about the crews from Voyager 3 and 4? When will we get to talk to them?"

"Only Voyager crew members will be made available for interviews," the NASA official bluntly replied.

"Which Voyager?" Yasmin asked.

"Voyager, or what the public commonly refers to as Voyager 5," the official answered.

"Right, but what about 3 and 4?"

"As you can imagine, their bodies have been through quite a shock upon reentry," the official answered. "It will take some time before they acclimate themselves enough to be able to come in contact with the general public."

Yasmin was persistent. "What about written communication?" she asked. "Can I provide a list of questions for the first Voyager crews to respond to?"

The NASA official paused, and after conferring for a moment with another NASA member, she replied, "Yes, that would be acceptable."

The NASA officials abruptly thanked the media and ended the briefing as reporters continued shouting questions at their backs as they retreated behind the curtain.

Yazmin couldn't believe her good luck. It wasn't an in-person interview, and it was unlikely she would ever actually see the people she was interviewing, but it was something. The rest of the reporters might be satisfied with access to Voyager 5 and the official statements that NASA would offer about the crews of Voyager 3 and 4, but not Yazmin. She was most curious about the difficult questions that probably wouldn't make it to the news and that her producer would likely cut. Reporting, for her, was a balance of doing enough of the job to maintain employment and using the access her position afforded her to satisfy her natural curiosity.

15—FROM THE PERSONAL RECORDS OF YASMIN'S INTERACTIONS WITH VOYAGER CREW MEMBERS

Transcript from my interview with Ms. Opal Watts

Yasmin: Ms. Watts, I need to start by saying you are my hero, and a hero to many other young girls and women around the world. How does it feel, to not only be the oldest living person, but also the only crew member to survive from the first Voyager flight?

Opal: Thank you for the kind words. It's a technicality, but just to make sure the record is straight, it should be Dr. Watts. I am glad that I can give hope to so many women out there. I was a girl with a dream, and I fought to make it possible, but, honestly, a lot of it was luck. I was at the right place at the right time, and caught the eye of the right people. It helped that I didn't have much of a family, or kids of my own. I'm sure that part isn't inspiring, but it's the truth. You can fight all you want and do everything you can to stack the deck in your favor, but luck will always play a huge role. You can't see me shrugging my shoulders, but that's my response to being the oldest person alive. Keep putting one foot in front of another, take another breath, live another day. My quality of life right now isn't great, hooked up to all these machines, but I am alive to see all the things that have been accomplished while we were away. Being the last member of Voyager 3 makes me sad more than anything else. They were my family, and I was there when each one of them passed.

Yasmin: Can you speak to the stories about Amelia Gardner, Kirk, Eva, and Edgar?

Opal: What stories? I have plenty.

Yasmin: About their passing.

Opal: Like I said earlier, with respect to luck playing a role in my ending up on Voyager 3, luck plays a huge role in how long we live. Everyone has a clock, and it's just a matter of time. Some are up sooner than others. I have fond memories of all of them, but Amelia most of all. She was a special woman, a lot like a sister to me. I miss her every day.

Yasmin: She passed in 2043, right?

Opal: Thirty-four years ago.

Yasmin: What kind of Commander was Hugh Sullivan? It seems like from what we've heard that he was a divisive figure. Was that true?

Opal: Hugh was a measured, focused man. He was married to the mission, and he did everything in his power to ensure it was successful.

Yasmin: Did it ever put you and him at odds?

Opal: If you've ever been in a long-term relationship, you know every couple has a disagreement from time to time. Heck, even the people I love the most drive me nuts if I can't have a little space. I mean, room. I don't know anyone who doesn't need a little away time. But, up there, in Voyager, we didn't exactly have a lot of room. There was no such thing as "me time." So, yeah, Hugh rubbed me the wrong ways at times. I think the biggest difference was he was a letter-of-the-law kind of guy, and I was much more the intent-of-the-law, or big picture type person. We both believed in the mission; we just saw different ways to arrive at the destination.

Yasmin: Can you say more about that? What kind of differences?

Opal: We had a manual and a set of procedures. That was Hugh's bible. I figured, once we were out of Earth's orbit, that we had a little wiggle-room to find our own groove. It wasn't like NASA was going to check-in on us. For me, when an issue came up, I thought it was appropriate that we discuss our options. But Hugh always turned to the manual and found some wording he believed to be relevant. That was probably our biggest disagreement. He'd say, "It's right here on page 37," and I'd counter with, "That book was written by people who theorized what this would be like and have never left Earth before." The rest of the team, originally just Arnold and Amelia but then later the rest, Kirk, Rebecca, Sidney, and so on, they usually agreed with me. Hugh was the kind of person that didn't take kindly to being second-guessed, and with the NASA bible as his defense and his rank of Commander on his side, he almost always got his way. I know I shouldn't speak ill of the dead, but frankly, I always had the sense that Hugh would never relinquish control of Voyager, that he'd hold onto some vital piece of information until the bitter end and then doom the rest of us by dying with that knowledge. Fortunately, we never got to that point.

Yasmin: Wow. I had no idea he was such a tyrant.

Opal: Tyrant is a bit harsh, but you get the idea.

Yasmin: Is there any way you can provide me with a copy of the manual or the set of procedures? I'd love to see what kind of rule book you were working with.

Notes to self

Instead of a response from Opal, there has been silence, and then today I received a notification from NASA that Opal Watts passed away. Opal Watts was almost one hundred thirty years old, and her body had been through a lot, but her death has taken me by surprise. I had naively assumed Opal would live on. I find myself grieving the loss of never meeting Opal in person.

I've been asked to speak at the national memorial in honor Opal Watts.

Today at Opal's memorial I received a message from Isiah Heller.

Transcript from my interview with Mr. Isiah Heller, brother to Freddy Heller

Yasmin: Mr. Heller, thank you for reaching out to me.

Isiah: You're welcome. But I have to admit to having somewhat selfish reasons for doing so. I want to talk to my brother, Freddy Heller, but apparently, we are only allowed to communicate to selected members of the press. Opal said nice things about you, so I figured I'd trust you, too.

Yasmin: I'm happy to help however I can. What can I do?

Isiah: Well, first I'd like to know if Freddy Heller is still alive. If he isn't, I want to know what happened, to read his obituary or whatever else there is about his life. If he is still alive, then I want him to know that his big brother loves him and misses him. I never stopped missing him.

Yasmin: I can definitely do that. Would you be willing to tell me more about your experiences on Voyager 4? I was working with Opal, but I want to interview everyone from the different Voyagers about their experiences.

Isiah: Sure. Not much to say though. We went up and floated through space until a more sophisticated ship rendered our mission futile.

Yasmin: I'm more interested in the day-to-day. How you became involved with the mission in the first place. What the dynamics were like aboard the ship. That kind of thing.

Isiah: You get me the information about my brother, and I'll bore you all day with the details.

Post Interview Notes with Mr. Heller
It didn't take long me long to find what Isiah wanted. Fredrick Heller was dead. I don't know the best way to tell him. It shouldn't be a surprise to Isiah, because he himself is one hundred and nine. His "little" brother was eleven years younger, but had he survived, Freddy would have been ninety-eight years old. It seems he lived a good, long life, but he didn't have the benefit of being isolated in space with the reprieve from Earth's gravity pulling on him. I'll do my best to reconstruct Freddy's life for Isiah, but Freddy wasn't a celebrity or a person of interest. This is going to be difficult. There are relatively few sources to work with. It would help if Freddy had married or had any living family members.

I sent a letter to Isiah with the little information I could find on Freddy.

Today I received a note from Isiah that simply said "thank you."

It's been two weeks with no further communication from Isiah. I'm considering reaching out again.

Today a letter finally arrived.

Letter from Mr. Isiah Heller
Isiah: I've thought about how to reply, but honestly, I don't know what to say. It's like I said earlier, we floated through space. We looked out our portholes, we read, we played games. We were bored out of our minds. There was nothing, literally nothing. We took readings and gathered data, but after a while that was useless because we had no way to convey that information back to Earth. When Joanna refused to have more children after having Omar, it was the end of the mission. I resigned myself to dying in space, and I'm sure the others did, too. We didn't talk about it. We are all scientists; we knew the outcome if no new females were produced for the longevity of the mission. There wasn't much more to do on board other than think about the possibilities. I was constantly reminded of my mortality. After Omar was born and Joanna said she was done, that was it. It was just a matter of time. I considered stepping out into space a number of times. It would have been painful, but it would have been over quicker than waiting for nature to take its course on board. Hell, how long did Hugh live? Into his hundred-thirties? And that was only because he came to Earth; who knows how much longer we would have lived up there. Now, what? I'm back on Earth, but now what? NASA can poke and prod me and learn all about how space and radiation effects the human body, but what about my actual quality of life? What do I get for my time served? I was thirty-three when we launched, which means I spent two-thirds of my life in space. Spent it in a tube with people I barely knew when we started. And now, here I am, back on Earth, and I don't even have those people around me. I'm surrounded by people I don't know checking in and asking me questions who are interested in data, not Isiah Heller. Scientifically, I understand it. They need to do tests; they want to understand;

they need to make sure I won't spread some kind of space-borne virus. They need to protect me, for my own safety, against whatever germs have grown on Earth since I left. I get it, I really do, but it doesn't make it any easier to deal with it. At least Zina and me, and Nelda and Jolanda are old enough we won't have to worry about this much longer. But, what about Salvador? Or Joanna? Or the last generation from Voyager 3? Or baby Omar? That kid is only seven. What will his life be like? Will Joanna be able to get a job and support herself? This is the kind of shit that I can't help but think about. You want a story? It's not about what happened up there; it's about what happens now that we're back.

Notes to Self

This is an angle I haven't considered: Reintegration. Isiah is right. We've been too focused on what happened up there and ignored where things go from here. I need to reach out to the younger crewmembers from Voyager 3: Maggie (43), Kelvin (11), Kacey (11), and to Joanna (40) from Voyager 4. While I'm interested in Omar's future, I don't know that contacting a seven-year old is worth my time at this point.

The twins have responded and want to talk. I have not heard back from Joanna (and honestly, I don't expect to). I have an interview set up with Maggie later this month. This will be interesting.

Notes from Interview with Kelvin and Kacy

They weren't like any eleven-year-olds I have ever spoken with. Their vocabulary was so elevated, and they had no sense of the general playfulness that kids on Earth have. It made sense; they had been raised to be scientists to take on the burden of the mission from the moment they were born. Still, this was a surprising interview. I didn't always know how to respond.

Transcript from Interview with Kelvin and Kacy

155

Kelvin: I've heard about Earth, and I've seen bits and pieces of it on the various screens, but I don't know what to expect. What should my life be like? What should I want now that I'm here?

Yasmin: <<verbal pause>>

Kacey: Whenever I have time to myself, I'm trying to learn more about this planet. It's so marvelous. The colors are so bright and there are so many different forms of life. You have no idea how simplistic our life was on Voyager. We were surrounded by nothing. We had each other, but that was about it. We learned about animals and plants, but I had no idea there would be so many of them. I just want to walk through a forest. That's really what I want.

Yasmin: I hope you can do that soon. I'm sure you'll be able to.

Kacey: I hope so. Do you know how much longer it will be? I keep asking, but they just keep saying, "Soon; we're almost done."

Yasmin: I really don't know. I wish I did. But, when you're done, I'd love to go with you on that walk through the forest. Did either of you ever see some kind of rule book? Opal told me about it.

Kelvin: We had a bunch of books, and I think I read them all. I don't remember a rule book.

Kacey: Same.

Notes to Self
I have spent the last couple of months getting to know Maggie. I think we're forming a kind of friendship. There is so much to learn, and I feel underprepared and inadequate to

carry these stories forward. I am going to keep working on this, even if it means my other projects suffer. I just feel compelled to understand!

Transcript from first interview with Maggie

Maggie: I just want a house one day, and a job and that stuff I read about in books. Do you think that's possible?

Yasmin: I can't imagine why not. You're still young. You have a lot of life ahead of you. I mean, they can't keep you forever. They're going to run out of tests and questions eventually. It's not like you've committed a crime. If they hold you much longer, you could always sue them.

Maggie: What do you mean?

Yasmin: It's a legal mechanism. You would charge NASA with holding you against your will, or sue them for false pretenses or something. I really don't know; I'm not a lawyer. But I would imagine you could get a class action lawsuit together.

Maggie: What would be the justification? Or why would a court hear my case?

Yasmin: Well, you didn't sign up for this. Right? I mean, you weren't one of the original crew members who signed their lives away and took off into space. You were born on the ship. You had no say. Seems like there would be a case there.

Maggie: Interesting. What could I get from that kind of trial?

Yasmin: I would imagine you'd get quite a bit. People sue for stupid shit all the time and win big. Freedom is one of those things we value down here, and you, and the rest of the people born in space, had no say in being part of that mission.

Of course. Hmm.

Maggie: What?

Yasmin: Well, I'm not sure if U.S. law would protect you because you were born in space. I mean, are you a U.S. citizen?

Maggie: I don't know. I'm in the United States now. Doesn't that make me a citizen?

Yasmin: Usually you have to be born in the United States or work to become a citizen. But, maybe the Voyager is considered a U.S. territory. That would make sense. And the egg and sperm used to conceive you were from U.S. citizens— I think, you might need to look into that. Did they keep records of whose eggs and sperm were used?

Maggie: I'm sure they kept records of what was used. We were meticulous and kept many journals and records.

Yasmin: Were you ever told anything about who your parents were?

Maggie: Parents?

Yasmin: I mean, the people who donated the sperm and egg? Is there like a file on those people to tell you about who you came from?

Maggie: No. At least none that I ever saw. That would be interesting to learn something about them. Do you think they're still alive?

Yasmin: No. They would have died a long time. Sorry.

Maggie: Could you find out who they were? I'd like to know.

Yasmin: I can try. Since the scandal, NASA has been pretty forthcoming.

Maggie: What scandal?

Yasmin: Well, your missions were kept secret from the public. And it was only through researchers like Troy Baines and Jackie King that we learned about the flights in the first place.

Maggie: Why did they keep the flights secret?

Yasmin: They haven't ever publicly said, but I imagine it's because they were afraid of what the public would say. Or think. The missions were experiments, and in general, people on Earth frown on experimenting with human lives. But they really wanted to test out their theories. In theory, it sounded like a good idea. In practice, not so much.

Maggie: Oh. We were just an experiment?

Yasmin: I'm sorry. That must make you feel like shit. But you were an experiment that worked. They were right about the theory. It could be done; it would just take a very long time.

Maggie: And mean that people like me, anyone born in between the launch and landing, were just there to produce and educate the next generation to keep the mission going.

Yasmin: Right. That's why the public would have been outraged. And, it's why I think you'd have a strong class action suit.

Notes to self – Three weeks after initial interview with Maggie
I don't know if NASA is monitoring my conversations or

whether it is simply a coincidence, but Maggie and the rest of the crew were released this morning. Each of them is being given a home, and the children have all been adopted by families. Not surprisingly, Isiah has refused NASA's housing and will be returning to life outside of the protective walls of NASA. He did accept some medical help though. His legs no longer support him, but NASA has provided robotic technology that makes it possible for him to walk. I've heard, but not yet confirmed, that other members born in space have similar struggles and will be given appropriate technology for reintegration to life on Earth.

Transcript from follow-up interview with Maggie
Yasmin: So, how do you like it?

Maggie: Like what?

Yasmin: Well, you have your house now, and you're all settled. What do you think about it?

Maggie: It's beautiful. I wonder why anyone would ever leave. I can't help but be frustrated by the years I wasted up there when there is so much richness down here. I am lonely though. I'm so used to having people with me all the time; I don't really know that I like being by myself. Will you come visit me?

Notes to self
I think I'm going to move in with Maggie. We plan to travel to Burma for a month.

Isiah killed himself. I just received a copy of the note he left behind. I am reluctant to tell Maggie.

Letter from Isiah
Hey,
I know that seems like a rather informal way to start a letter

like this, but how do you start one of these? Goodbye cruel world? Even I know that's cliché.

Funny to think about all that time up there and, now, home for such a short time, but it feels like forever. So much has changed. I remember playing the Atari for the first time, and thinking it was the coolest thing ever. Before that, you had to waste buckets of quarters at the arcade. The Atari brought it right home. It was great. There was something about those games; I really couldn't get enough. Some friends had the ColecoVision—that was the original home of Mario and Donkey Kong—and it had those crazy controllers with a knob and a number pad. Others had the Intellivision or the Odyssey. Each of them had some kind of learning curve, where you got used to the controls and how to operate them. I always felt like they were on the same basic level though.

I mean, there were plusses and minuses, but ultimately the graphics were very similar and the functionality was essentially the same. The first Sega and Nintendo were a monumental leap forward, but, even then, if you had played the one before, you could figure out the new systems. The Sega Genesis was my system. God, I loved that thing. The graphics were such a huge step up from what came before, but it felt comfortable and familiar.

Now though, I feel like I'm trying to translate playability from a console game to a computer. You know, trying to figure out how to use the keyboard to move, adapting the simple directional arrows or joystick into letters. I'm not doing a good job of this, I'm sorry. I just remember someone trying to show me how to play a racing game—I don't even remember what it was now—on the keyboard. It was a game I had played on the Sega before, and the friend was trying to show me how you could just use "e" to move forward and the spacebar for the gas. I was great on the console, but I could never make sense of it on the keyboard. It just didn't translate for me.

And now, I know all the kids say the games are great and the interface is supposed to be super easy, but I just don't get it. Something's missing and I haven't played each of the successive iterations of things to be able to make that progression to the next system. Does that make sense? (I realize there's no way you'll be able to answer, and yet I wrote that anyway.)

Besides, Freddy's gone. I miss him. Wish I could have one more day just to hear about his life.

Everyone I knew is gone. I mean, the family name lives on. I keep getting people reaching out to me, wanting this or that, thinking I'm made of money I guess, or hoping some of my "fame" will rub off on them. But no one I know. No one I feel any connection to.

Curiosity used to drive me and I always thought it would continue to do so. That I'd wonder, "what will happen today?" and that would be enough. Or that I'd want to see how the rest of the crew manages to adapt and move on. But, I'm old. Really old. Not as old as some, but old enough.

Rather than waiting for time to make its move, I'm going to call it a day and see what happens next. Logically, scientifically, deep in my bones, I suspect there's nothing. But you see enough of the universe and you start to wonder if there isn't some kind of design. On a very basic level, my atoms will live on. In another form, sure, but I like the idea that maybe the carbon that I'm made of will transfer to another living organism, or a star, or something. Carl Sagan said a thing or two about that.

Ending this letter is just as hard as starting it was, so I'll just say: see you in the ether.

~Isiah

Notes to self

I've been thinking a lot about Eloise and scouring interviews to see what the captain of Voyager 5 has already said. I need a new angle.

I had an aha moment today. Everyone has been asking

Eloise what it was like for her, this hero, to rescue the crews of these "lost" spaceships. They all want to know how she felt, what she saw, and how it felt to complete the mission. No one has asked her about the conversations she had with the Voyager 3 and 4 crews. This is my angle . . . I hope she'll do one more interview.

Transcript from my interview with Eloise
Eloise: We didn't have a lot of time to get to know them. They were clearly shaken by seeing humans after all that time. And I suppose our spacesuits looked futuristic to them. Not to mention our ship. Is that what you mean?

Yazmin: Not exactly. I'm more curious about how it felt. Did they see it as a rescue? Was it something they wanted? Was it a relief?

Eloise: Hard to say. Again, I didn't spend a lot of time with them, and it wasn't like we were just idling around chatting. But if it were me in their position, I think that would be a very difficult spot to be in. I got to complete my mission, but theirs was aborted. Of course, none of them would have lived to see the end of their mission in the first place, which for me, is really remarkable. That's the bravery that's underappreciated and not talked about. These people, they all agreed to leave everything they knew behind with no hope of seeing the completion of the mission. They all signed up to die in space. And yet, here we were, bringing them home.

Yazmin: Do you think they still thought of it as home?

Eloise: Well, most of them had never stepped foot on Earth before. Their entire reality was the ship. For them, I bet there was some measure of excitement and relief. For the others, the original crew members that had survived, I don't know. Clearly, they didn't have much they were leaving behind or had come to terms with leaving it in the past.

Yazmin: How do you feel about the label of hero? I've read and listened to—honestly, I don't remember how many—interviews, and every one of the people speaking to you calls you a hero. Do you see that?

Eloise: Hero is tricky word. I think a lot of people attribute "hero" to me because I did something that they wouldn't have. But really, my "leap of faith" was simply that this warp technology would work. We had tested it and we were 99% certain everything would go according to plan. I'm not a religious person, but I also understand that some people think of science as a sort of religion.

Yazmin: How do you mean?

Eloise: In that, at some point, you have to accept something that you, yourself didn't witness. You tell me there are atoms that make up everything, provide logic, and a solid argument, and I accept that. You tell me the Big Bang is what started the universe, walk me through how, answer some questions, and I believe. Religion isn't so different, there are just fewer "tests" and "validations." You ask me what I believe in, and I say science. That's what I believe in. Part of why I admire the scientific process is that it is constantly checking itself, verifying, and revalidating its conclusions. Anyway, all this is to answer your question about what a "hero" is. I know this will probably be unpopular, but it's what I believe. Firefighters, police officers, doctors, astronauts, we are not heroes. We are doing a job we signed up for. We knew exactly what we were getting into when we took this as our career. Does it require bravery to run into a burning building? Absolutely. Do I admire what firefighters do? One hundred percent. Are they a hero? I'd say no. Running into that burning building is literally their job. Me? Shooting off into space, that's what I get paid to do. Sure, it's not for everyone, but there are plenty of people who want to be astronauts. But that neighbor who flees a burning apartment building, makes it out safely and hears a crying baby or someone calling for help and runs back into that building? That person, who is just living his or her life and runs back into that building? That's a hero.

Yazmin: I like that. And I tend to agree. So, to quote you, astronauts are not heroes?

Eloise: I didn't quite say that. I don't see myself as a hero. I don't think of the Voyager 5 people as heroes. We all knew what we were signing up for, we had a national celebration of our launch, everyone was very clear about what we were doing. We will fly on other missions, and we will continue to be paid to do this work. But, the earlier crews? They signed up, but they never had any fanfare, never had any expectation of anyone knowing what they had accomplished, and were never compensated for their work. In my book, they are all heroes. Even the ones who didn't make it.

16—EARTH: DEATH OF BABY GROVER (2112)

When Grover died, Voyager 3 and Voyager 4 were far from home (890.6~ AU and 1,569.1~ AU respectively). The crew, the ones still living, were safely on Earth, but their spacecrafts were now still only a fraction of the distance toward their original destination. Even Voyager 4 had only accomplished 0.58% of its goal. Instead of drifting uselessly as space debris (like so many other abandoned probes were), they had become probes like their original namesakes. Traci Vargas and Casey Welch flew missions to convert them for a continued purpose. Newly retrofitted, Voyager 3 and Voyager 4 now had technology that the original crews couldn't have imagined. There were cameras, monitors, and listening devices to record all sorts of data. Each ship now also had a way to convey that information back home. While the information both ships gathered was studied, it was for posterity more than anything. NASA had crafts capable of traveling much further than any of the original four Voyagers ever would. Providing these updates was a way of keeping the original spirit of the mission alive.

Grover had also transformed over the years. He was born Grover Taft Baines and was immediately dubbed Baby Grover. He never really had a chance to enjoy his given name. Once he grew out of the baby-stage, he transitioned into a new nickname: Junior. He didn't mind so much, even though he had no tangible connection to his great grandfather. All the stories he heard about his namesake were favorable, but when people outside the family heard him called Junior, they asked about his father. This meant that Grover had to explain the origins of the nickname, and even if he didn't disclose anything, it was a reminder that he had never known his father.

"I don't know anything about him," was his standard answer, and it was mostly the truth. Grover knew that his father was an actual living being who had met his mother at some point and had procreated with her. His father was not selected from a database of attributes—though that option was available to his mother had she wished it. The truth was that Grover was a product of an "old fashion" date of meeting someone casually, finding that you share things in common with one another, having sex, and then failing to reconnect afterward. There was no dramatic parting of ways, or falling out, or divorce, or anything of the sort.

Secretly Troy and Rose were disappointed that Harper was a single mother, but in the end, the whole thing worked to their benefit. Their daughter moved home and their relationship blossomed into something that surprised everyone. When Baby Grover was born, the absent father failed to matter much. By the time Baby Grover—now Junior—asked the inevitable questions about his father, Harper could quite honestly shrug and say there wasn't much to tell.

Later when he finally chose to go by his given name and someone asked, "Grover, huh?" he'd answer with, "It's an old family name," and then redirect the conversation with, "My great grandfather used to work for NASA," and suddenly his namesake was far more interesting.

In many ways, Grover grew into his great grandfather's likeness without ever having met him. They resembled one another in many ways, but not in the way a son looks like a mini-version of his father. Instead, it was more in the hobbies and tastes that they shared. Baby Grover had an intense love of donuts. Harper once recalled pushing him in a cart at a grocery store when suddenly Baby Grover began grunting, "Nuh, nuh!" It took Harper a while to figure out what he meant. The first time she ignored it. The second time she thought it was peculiar. But, by the third time she had to find out what was going on.

"Nuh! Nuh!" Grover said.

"What? Where?" Harper asked.

Baby Grover pointed and continued with, "Nuh, nuh!"

Harper did her best to follow his lead. Eventually, she found herself at the bakery buying a donut for her son. How on earth did he know where the bakery was? As far as she knew, he'd never had donuts from the grocery store. And it wasn't like they were even remotely by the bakery when he started in with his, nuh-nuh'ing. The kid had a radar for fried dough.

Grover also had a love for ice-skating that no one could explain. It wasn't like Florida presented a lot of opportunities for ice-skating. There was the professional hockey team, and there were ice arenas, but the family never frequented them. Yet, when a friend had a birthday party at an ice rink, Junior surprised everyone by taking to the ice like a pro. He needed help lacing his skates—what kid doesn't?—but once laced, he hit the ice and had to be coerced to stop. Great Grandfather Grover was an Escanaba native so ice-skating was in his blood.

The Grovers shared a name, love of donuts, ice-skating, and other obscure loves that were harder to dismiss, like their attractions to Joan Miro paintings, the music of Wendy Carlos, and the Brutalist architecture movement. None of these things could be easily explained because Great Grandfather Grover had been dead for thirty-two years by the time Baby Grover was born in 2011. It wasn't like the grandparents or his mother made a point of playing Carlos' *Sonic Seasonings* or the soundtrack to *A Clockwork Orange*, or took him to museums with impressive collections of Spanish experimental art, or admired concrete, blocky buildings. And yet, when they happened to tour the campus of Southern Illinois University, Carbondale, Junior perked up and pointed out a building.

"Look at that," he said.

"Ew," his mother said. It looked like a lump of cement.

Undeterred, Grover went over to Faner Hall and admired the different angles and aesthetic. When he returned to his mother's side he said, "Yep, definitely Brutalist. Beautiful, isn't it?" She raised an eyebrow and then changed the subject. Every campus they went to seemed to have some building in that style, and Grover was strangely drawn to them.

Once school was done and his career established, after he moved out on his own and he was married, Grover fully grew into his given name. Clifton, his husband, loved the name—it was actually the reason they met. They were both at the same social function. Clifton had already been there long enough to have a drink in hand and was making the rounds when suddenly a newcomer arrived. Clifton noticed, but the newcomer didn't really have his attention until he heard the man's name. At least, he thought he had heard it right. There was a fair amount of noise and he couldn't be sure. He made his way around the room and touched the man on his shoulder.

"Excuse me," Clifton said. "Did you say your name is Grover?"

"I did." Had Grover been younger, he might have winced or tried to redirect the conversation or even to fill the silent void that followed his answer, but he had reached the point in his life where he was old enough to be tired of games or hiding or talking for the sake of filling the air. He waited to see what this other man would do.

"It's an amazing name," Clifton said. "I love it." He, too, was now past the point of games or trying to impress anyone. He smiled and waited in comfortable silence to see what would happen next.

Grover surprised himself then by doing the thing everyone had always asked for but that he rarely would indulge anyone in. He became animated and screamed, "NEAR!" in Clifton's face, and then ran across the room stopping with an exaggerated stutter and screamed, "FAR!" He now had the room's attention. Grover ran back over to Clifton, nearly tripping over his shoes before grazing the man's nose with his own and whispering, "near" into his face. The room erupted into laughter. Everyone wanted to tell Grover how hilarious he was, and how funny the impression had been, but he only had ears for Clifton. Somehow, amid the music and conversations and general loudness of the party, the two had an intimate conversation and fell in love.

When they discussed having children, Grover made it clear that all parents would be in the picture.

"What do you mean?" Clifton asked.

"It's not that I regret not knowing my father, but I think it's important that kids have the opportunity to know who helped produce them," Grover said. "Even if it's purely for health reasons."

"How's that going work? Can't we just provide our kids with health records and genetic testing?"

"We'll just need to be selective about our surrogates," said Grover. He put his arm around Clifton. "Beyond looking at the obvious attributes we might select, let's also look for compatibility. It would be pretty cool to be in a long-term relationship with the people who end up creating our kids."

"Okay," said Clifton. He didn't object to having a larger family. Both he and Grover came from fairly small families, and now their "family" was primarily made of a circle of friends. It wouldn't hurt to increase the size of it a little more. "Got anyone in mind?"

Grover didn't, and the prospects of going to a clinic to choose from a binder of possibilities didn't seem in the spirit of the mothers being part of the experience. The conversation stalled there as they went about doing dishes and shifted their attention to preparing for the next day.

That next day found Clifton at his favorite coffee shop. He was enjoying an espresso while watching life happen around him. Usually he blocked out the sounds of the coffeehouse to let his mind meander wherever it might, but today he found his mind a jumbled mess and instead distracted himself from those thoughts by eavesdropping on the conversations around him. He was sitting at the front of the store, and so there were a number of occupied tables behind him.

A one-sided conversation was occurring on a phone at one table, "Monday works. Yes. What about three?"

Another table was covered with papers and the woman sitting there was talking to herself as she worked, "The data from Table 7.2 and then the quote from page 38, and I'll combine it with…" But that didn't interest Clifton.

Instead, his ears settled on the only conversation he could hear both side of. Two young women, maybe twenty-two, he wasn't sure, each held a coffee mug, but neither was drinking it. It was clear they had come for the conversation and companionship; the coffee was only the pretense that brought them together.

"I really don't know what I'll do," the darker-skinned one said. "The degree is useless on its own. I need to keep going to school."

"But how long can you afford to do that?" the one with glasses asked. "I mean, you can't spend your life in school. Even if you'd want to." She laughed and lifted the mug to her lips, but instead of drinking it, she just held it there.

"Right. I can't stay in school forever and, financially, I couldn't afford to anyway."

"Have you looked for assistantships or grants?" The heat from her coffee was beginning to steam her glasses.

"I have, but there's no guarantee." She sighed and turned her coffee mug in her hand. "I just need a rich uncle. Stacy, do you have one of those I can borrow?"

Stacy laughed. "I wish." She lowered her mug to the table. "You could always sell something."

"I doubt selling my used textbooks is going to get me very far, plus if I keep going to school, I'll just need more of those anyway." She paused. "I keep droning on about me, but what about you?"

"I'm in the same place you are. Consider this both therapy

and research," Stacy laughed.

Clifton turned from facing the window and approached their table. "I couldn't help but hear your dilemma."

"Are you my long-lost rich uncle?" the woman without glasses asked.

"Or mine?" Stacy asked. "Angel investor?"

"I don't think we're related," Clifton laughed and gestured at the chair. "May I join you?"

The women nodded, and he slid into the seat.

"I'm Clifton," he said.

"Stacy."

"And I'm Lyvia."

Clifton smiled at them both. "I don't know how to say without sounding a little," he struggled for the right word. "I don't know. So, I'll just say it." He spoke quickly so they wouldn't have an opportunity to interrupt before he finished. "My husband, Grover, and I would like to have a big family. Would either, or both of you, be interested in surrogacy? We'd pay well, but it's more than that. Because, we'd want you to be involved in the lives of the children."

And here Lyvia interrupted, "Involved? Like how? As mothers? Because I'm not ready for that. If you were listening, I want to go to school." Stacy wasn't sure what she wanted from life, but thought Lyvia's question was a good one. She turned her head to see what Clifton had to say in response.

"Honestly, it's more my husband's thing, and I'm not sure I fully grasp it, but I'll do my best. He never knew his father, and he wants to make sure his children at least have the opportunity to know everyone involved in their conception. It doesn't mean you need to live with us, but it means you'll always be welcome at the house, that you'll be invited for birthday parties and holidays, and that the children, when they get older, might want to spend time with you. I don't know, I don't really know that anyone will know how it will go until we try it."

"I like the idea of a big fluid family," Stacy said.

"We'll be able to be control the throttle of involvement

though, right?" asked Lyvia. "I mean, there's no obligation, or expectation, just the promise of being open to the children reaching out to us," she paused and raised her eyes squarely to Clifton's, "right?"

"Right. No contract, no forced visitation, just an openness and willingness."

"And you'll pay for our education?" asked Lyvia.

"I don't know that we've talked all that through yet, but we'll definitely be able to help, a lot," said Clifton. How much was a graduate education these days? He honestly didn't know.

Stacy shifted her attention to her friend, "Some is better than none."

"For sure," said Lyvia. "But pregnancy is going to control your life for at least a good portion of nine months."

"Right," said Stacy. "You could take a semester off, or time it to happen over the summer."

Clifton's head volleyed back and forth from Lyvia and Stacy as they discussed the possibilities.

"Summer is a terrible time to be all fat and pregnant," said Lyvia.

"Well, you can't have it all," said Stacy. "I mean, either time it during the hot time, or take a semester off, or juggle classwork around it. You don't have many other offers for free education."

"Let's say discounted until we've worked out the details," Clifton interjected.

"Will this make us like in-laws, or something?" asked Stacy. "No, that's from marriage. And children who share one parent are half-siblings, but what does that make us?"

Lyvia wasn't sure, and she shook her head, but she liked the deal Clifton proposed more and more. "I need to meet your husband before we work out any details, but I think we have a deal."

That Saturday, the doorbell rang and Grover answered the door. Introductions were made, and as he took their coats, Lyvia asked, "Is that 10,000 Maniacs?" Grover was impressed. The record predated his own birth by almost two decades, and this woman was clearly younger than him.

"Are you a fan?" he asked.

"More a Natalie Merchant fan than a 10,000 Maniacs fan," Lyvia answered. "But yeah."

"*Wishing Chair, In My Tribe, Blind Man's Zoo,* or *Our Time in Eden?*" he asked.

"Truthfully, I first heard the *MTV Unplugged* album and so that's always had a soft spot in my heart, but my favorite actual album is *In My Tribe.* You?"

They were off and running as if two old friends.

Two months later, Clifton and Grover had their sperm spun, and Stacy was impregnated using that cocktail. Lyvia needed time to finish up a sequence of classes before committing to being pregnant. The result, two days preterm, were the twins Lyle and Adrian. Then, when the twins were six months old, Lyvia was impregnated, resulting in Natalie. Two years later, Lyvia gave birth to Chester and Horace, bringing the Clifton-Grover total to five. With five kids under the age of five, the couple decided they were done, which was convenient because Stacy and Lyvia had found relationships of their own and were ready to move on and perhaps have a family of their own.

The idea that Grover impressed upon them, to always remain in contact with one another, resulted in an enormous extended family of blood-relatives and chosen family. It was a non-traditional set-up for sure, but because it was so important to all involved, only partners willing to accept the non-conventional family format were welcomed in, and the family grew and grew. This is why Grover's hospital bed, in 2112, ended up being surrounded by so many adoring onlookers. The room, literally, overflowed with humans. Lyle and Adrian were both there with their respective families, Natalie and her husband and their brood, Chester and Horace with their respective offspring, and also Lyvia and Stacy and everyone that had emerged from their relationships. Grover smiled hummed softly to himself.

Clifton leaned in close, inconspicuously hungry for a last

moment of intimacy with his life partner. "What are you saying, my love?" he whispered in Grover's ear.

Instead of answering, Grover continued humming.

The tune was familiar, but Clifton couldn't quite place it. He knew he'd heard it before, definitely. That much was certain, but his husband was always more into music than he was. He asked again, "What is it? What song is that?"

Grover smiled. As much as Grover wanted to answer him, he couldn't quite bring himself to talk before the end of the song. He tried harder to clearly sing the words for Clifton to identify the song "I've Lost the Very Best of Me."

That was enough. Clifton understood the message as tears began to run down cheek. And then Grover was gone. He passed surrounded by a constellation of people who loved him, from his children and grandchildren and great grandchildren, to gestational carriers and their families, to friends, to his life partner and true love – all radiating out from his hospital bed. Instead of going supernova, he simply blinked and was gone.

EPILOGUE

The Alpha-Centauri-bound Voyager vessels continued on without their human cargo through the darkness, while their human cargo struggled to find meaning on Earth. By now, Salvador, and Joanna were in the mid-to-late-seventies, Kelvin and Kacey both mid-forties, and baby Omar forty-two, but as much as they shared in common with their Earth-born humans—chromosomes and genes, struggles with identity and aging, desire for companionship and relationships—they were primarily seen as purely alien. They were beings from space that had landed and now walked the surface of the planet. Only Maggie seemed to escape that cycle, though she had her moments of sadness and inner toil as well.

The true heart-break was baby Omar. He had been so young when he landed on Earth that everyone assumed he would integrate into society without any difficulty. Sadly, it wasn't the case. Kids are cruel, and Omar never quite found a path to fit in. He begged and pleaded with NASA to send him on other missions, but he lacked the physique necessary to be an astronaut. His legs never quite developed to adapt to Earth's gravity, and his body struggled in other ways. He was short, which was actually a selling point for astronauts due to the cramped conditions onboard, but there were no ways around other physical regulations. Astronauts must be fit and strong, not differently fit or differently strong. NASA's shortsightedness didn't remember that Omar would be weightless and his legs wouldn't be an issue in space.

As we wrap up our journey, we need to check in with Eloise Fisher, Commander of the Voyager 5, the rescue mission and all that occurred after. She's seventy, and she's talking to a much younger commander. They are gazing at a star map of what is now the known universe. She turns to the man and can't remember his name. "Where do we go?" she asks. The man begins to point at unexplored galaxies, and Eloise lets her mind wander. She surveys all the trillions and trillions of stars. Just where do you go? Where do you start? Where do you begin to start? Even with travel being what it is now—it taking so, relatively little time—it still takes *time*. It's a project that will never end. The man is still speaking, but Eloise doesn't seem to notice.

"We see supernova in the sky every night," she says.

The man stops what he's saying and looks at her. She has his full attention.

"That's what I remember Neil DeGrasse Tyson saying once."

"Sure," the man says. "Of course."

"In the same breath, he pointed out that supernova are rare. But, because there are one hundred billion galaxies, the sample size becomes big enough that rare things become common."

The man waits for something more to come, but nothing does.

Eloise is thinking about whether rare or common, the stars and galaxies are wondrous things, but this mission, borne out of curiosity and wonder, has somehow been distilled to checking items off a list for this man and people like him. To explore is certainly noble, but can't they see the futility of the sheer scale they're up against? How many centuries will it take before they even make an infinitesimal dent on their to-do list? Fuel, ships, and resources are limited, and their quest is not. Her gaze turns back to the star map and rests on the Milky

Way. She looks and wonders, just where are the Voyagers?

Right where they'll also be: Little brother trailing bigger brother in perpetual motion. Both probes blink into the void, years and years from their established destinations. They were never programmed to land, and without a crew, they never will. Once the ships accomplish their missions, they will continue beyond Alpha Centauri until their energy sources fail and something interrupts their forward momentum. Voyager 4 will fail first. If it had a crew, they might have been able to keep it functioning. But the simplicity of Voyager 3 is its ticket to near-eternal life. Blink. Blink.

AUTHOR'S NOTE

First, thank you to Gayle, Dylan, and Parker. You're always very patient with me and enthusiastically encourage me pursuing my dreams.

Thank you also to my wonderful editor, collaborator, friend, and sometimes co-author, Heidi Wall Burns. Thanks also to the assist from Matt. You both always make my writing better.

Thanks also to my early readers (a different Matt, Paul, and Dan); your thoughts, feedback, and suggestions are always extremely helpful and very much appreciated.

This book began as a pipedream on July 23, 2014 at 1:19pm. I sent myself an email with the following message: "Three books: the first one begins in 1976, then maybe 1990 for book 2, and 2048 for the third when documents are declassified and a conspiracy theorist finally puts it all together and realizes how futile the missions were."

Hardly anything brilliant, eh?

I only share this here because this is typically my process. I get an idea and I email it to myself for "later use." Most of those story ideas die on the vine, but this one kept popping up at various times. In August of that year, I actually wrote 3,007 words. Some of it is "story" and the rest consists of rambling notes about the framework or what it might look like. I kept at it here and there and eventually it grew into a solid draft with several Excel spreadsheets (to track dates, time, distance, ages, etc.) in 2018. Which was reworked and revised multiple times.

Then 2020 happened. The isolation the characters dealt with really made this project feel urgent, and I kept working on it. Everything felt more pressing, because of the pandemic and being stuck in the house, and instead of waiting to share the books I had been writing, I decided: screw it. I sent Bidding Wars to Heidi and published it in May. Then I kept at Voyager.

Now, a few days after my 45th birthday, here it is. Ready for the presses. (Or whatever passes for those these days.) I won't formally release it until October 1st, because I want its publication to coincide with NASA's 62nd anniversary.

I never wanted to be an astronaut, but space has always fascinated me. Mary Roach's book *Packing For Mars* is fantastic and it helped me better conceptualize what space travel would be like. I share a sense of humor and curiosity with Mary Roach, and I hope some of that has come through in this quirky little sci-fi book.

Thanks for reading.

ABOUT THE AUTHOR

Michael MacBride has delivered newspapers, worked for UPS, delivered pizzas, done collections at a bank, was a roadie for a country band, was a grant-writer and funder-researcher for non-profits, taught English, Literature, and Humanities courses at universities and colleges in Minnesota, New Hampshire, Ohio, and Illinois, and held a few other jobs in between.

He has always been a reader and a writer.

Though originally from Michigan, his family calls Minnesota home.

Made in the USA
Monee, IL
03 October 2020

43877522R00111